spuds

by Paul Shriner

1

Tuberous Gladiators

By prevailing over all obstacles and distractions, one may unfailingly arrive at his chosen goal or destination.
- Christopher Columbus

Hip-high in mashed potatoes, two tuberous caped gladiators dressed in Mexican wrestling masks could not see as they fought off tears through their masks. They squared off in a ring for an old-fashioned rasslin' match. Both men knew that this event may be the end of an era.

Owyhee Kenny lurched forward and grabbed Big Doug. He thrust his head straight down into the silky mash of potato goo.

Big Doug, holding his breath, reached both arms forward, grabbed Owyhee Kenny by the ankles, and yanked until he fell flat on his back. Rasslers can't get traction in the pit, so Big Doug was just lucky to get his breath and reset.

The rasslin' match took place each year in Blackfoot, Idaho. Owyhee Kenny and Big Doug, both perennial favorites, were in the semi-finals again. The sponsor of the festival, the Southeast Idaho Potato Council was strong-arming the local-farmers. They wanted to own all of the potato farms in Blackfoot.

Owyhee Kenny and Big Doug were both seasoned rasslers and took it seriously. They had Mexican-wrestling, Lucha-Libre-like personalities to go along with their custom masks and capes.

Both men were top "spuds" in their bracket and had easily defeated out-of-towners who had shown up for the event and signed up to rassle in a drunken haze.

Surprisingly, mash potato rasslin' takes skill. This is the primary reason that the same rasslers appear in the finals each year.

Whoever wins the open class takes home the title of "Masher." That person is treated like royalty. The Masher wins free donuts and coffee at the Kwik-e-mart, a reserved parking spot at the Tatertown Market, and a picture hung up in City Hall alongside rows of past mashed potato rasslin' semi-final champions.

The picture hung each year for the last ten years had been the same person, Owyhee Kenny. He is a local potato farmer with a knack for a couple of traditional wrestling holds that perfectly adapt to the venue of creamed taters.

His nickname, Owyhee? In 1819, Fur-trapper Donald McKenzie named the Owyhee Mountain after the Hawaiian Islands. Three of his men were lost to the "wilderness." McKenzie was a better friend than he was a speller, as the range has been misspelled ever since.

Owyhee Kenny, in his childhood, was nicknamed after that same mountain range.

PRO TIP: There are 2,755 miles between the Hawaiian Islands and the Owyhee Mountains, as the crow flies.

Nervous energy from the crowd hung over the ring. The announcer spoke in his microphone. No one could hear him. The hooting and hollering was so loud.

Both men kissed the giant chicken-wire framed potato as they entered the ring with songs from the movie Rocky, "Getting Stronger" and "Eye of the Tiger."

The crowd was pumped. The songs and spectacle set the electric tone. Through the whole match, the energy of the crowd never dimmed. Both men were covered in potato mash head to toe. There is no "pinning" in potato rasslin', the only way out of the pit is to eliminate yourself, or quit. The match is a marathon and not a sprint. It is not uncommon for a match to take up to an hour.

Everyone in Blackfoot loves the event except one person, Sparky. He was the head of the Southeast Idaho Potato Council. Sparky didn't like potatoes, the city of Blackfoot or this festival. He only cared about one thing, winning. His battle and victory was to gain control of every potato farm in the community.

This year during the event, Sparky was at the back of the crowd, the very back. After a couple of minutes, he looked around and noticed that everyone was watching the event.

Everyone.

Sparky noticed a truck just up a slight

slope idling. It had delivered all of the potatoes for the event. The driver had left it running. Sparky noticed that the nose of the truck was pointed right at the rasslin' ring. A fiendish grin attacked his face.

Sparky wanted to own all of the farms in the area. The two rasslers just happened to be the only two people left who still owned their farms. If he were able to interrupt the match, with that truck, the morale of the community might be destroyed. The tragedy could create a fire sale on potato farms.

Getting caught didn't matter for Sparky. Corruption was so rampant that SIPC basically owned all of the police, judges, and attorneys in town.

Like all good literary villains, Sparky was not just a bad guy who likes to steal potato farms from innocent farmers, he was a wealthy, scheming, selfish autocrat.

Everyone has a dark side. Sparky's wasn't just dark, it was black and hardened like obsidian.

From the passenger side of the truck, outside the view of most people, Sparky put on leather gloves. He did this to remove any of his fingerprints from the "accident" that he was about to create. He climbed into the cab of the truck, crossed the long bench seat, released the parking brake.

As soon as the truck started to roll ever so slowly, Sparky jumped out the passenger door and disappeared from view.

The truck rolled along building inertia. Gradually people in the crowd were beginning to notice the truck was rolling and getting faster. The truck consumed the food court like a tornado hitting a trailer park. It was now dead-nuts aimed at center ring.

There was Pandamonium, everyone ran. Chaos, people fell over and were then helped back to their feet. This truck was not going to stop at just destroying the food court!

The rasslers noticed that there was a large truck heading right for them. They slopped out of the ring covered in the mash. They watched as a hurricane of steel and rubber crashed through the pit of potatoes. The madness eventually wrapping itself around a cement pole directly outside the Idaho Potato Museum. Bits of potato carnage, steel, rubber, and concrete were scattered everywhere.

Sparky decided to arrive at the scene angry-screaming, "What happened here? It looks like a Tornado came through."

The officer responded, "We're not sure, the truck, the trailer, and the festival are destroyed."

Sparky replied, "How does a truck just start driving and destroy an entire festival without anyone noticing?"

The officer responded, "Sir, we don't know. It could be foul play. At this point, there are no credible leads. Everyone was watching the potato rasslin', myself included. Listen, we know that the Potato Council is a huge sponsor and have a lot riding on this event and I want you to know that we will do everything that can be done to apprehend those responsible for this abominable action. I wouldn't be honest with you though if I told you that we had any leads."

There were two major sponsors, the Southeast Idaho Potato Council, and Betta-Cola, an Idaho-based soft-drink that had been on the national stage for decades.

Sparky raised an eyebrow and said, "Listen, I know that the department works very hard and you will do everything humanly possible to fix this. Was there no surveillance footage anywhere?"

To which the officer responded, "There isn't anything, there aren't cameras anywhere and no one knows a thing, yet, but we are going to keep looking, sir!"

Sparky weighed his words, "This hurts our community and the Potato Council, but we have been through worse, and always come back stronger than before."

Sparky walked away. He knew that he had gotten away with it. He walked past both rasslers dressed pitifully in Mashed Potatoes. He looked the titans directly in the eye.

Owyhee Kenny looked at Big Doug, and said, "This is going to hurt the community. Things were already bad, this are gonna get worse, way, way worse."

Doug replied, "You have no idea. We are buried. We literally don't have two potatoes to rub together right now. How is Dorothea doing with all of this Are you meeting with Sparky next week?."

"Yup, there are just two meetings this year, mine and yours. As for Dorothea, she is fine, I mean, she is anxious about life. She is having trouble sleeping. I haven't shared much with her as I don't want her to worry. She knows

what is going on, she has to." said Owyhee
Kenny.

Big Potato

I learned then that practically no one in the world is entirely bad or entirely good, and that motives are often more important than actions.

-Eleanor Roosevelt

Monday morning, Sparky had meetings scheduled with both farmers. The accident at the festival should have created enough additional confusion to remove any last shred of community morale.

Potato farmers had sold their homesteads one by one to Big Potato a.k.a. the SIPC. No one could do anything about it. Some folks were discouraged. They moved away and took jobs elsewhere for a higher wage. Others stayed and took lower paying jobs while working other people's' farms.

Each year, Big Potato would strong-arm the farm owners. They would send out a letter requesting a meeting. The farmer took the meeting or wouldn't be able to sell potatoes at market.

Big Potato controlled every aspect of the potato farming industry. You worked with the same people from seed to sale. If you sell potatoes, you take the meeting with the SIPC.

In Blackfoot, ID potato farmers own one suit. That suit is used for weddings, funerals and for this annual meeting with Big Potato. The farmer would show up to a very professional-looking business park. The kind of place scattered across America. Everything symmetrical and austere.

The tiny strips of lawn separate the building from the parking. The lawn is freshly cut, grass still laying down making a pattern. The Sprinklers spread drops of water. Lights escape the windows from the bank of neon lights obsessively ordered. Identical red doors sat atop a stairwell with exactly five steps.

Owyhee Kenny had just parked in his beat-up blue farm truck. Chompers, his dog, got out of the truck and waited by the door faithfully.

As Owyhee Kenny got to the lobby, Big Doug was leaving. The two men made eye contact. Big Doug immediately turned his gaze. His eyes were welling with tears. It was subtle, but it was clear. Big Doug was walking away from his life of farming. Owyhee Kenny had a lot of questions but knew that this was not the time nor place to get answers.

Owyhee Kenny entered the double doors, the receptionist greeted him. She asked for his name, even though she knew him very well. She gestured for Owyhee Kenny to take a seat in the waiting area. Sometimes farmers wait all day on chairs and couches exquisitely set in rows. There are no magazines but there is one book, George Washington of Centralia. It was not about the first president, but the founder of a tiny town in Washington State.

There are chairs, and a gray clock that hangs on the wall, just a bit askew. There is a sign to the right of the clock that says, "The eyes of the potato are always watching you." This sign was hung in the SIPC in several places. It was a marketing campaign that was launched to encourage employees to always do their best. There was an intended duality to the sign that wanted you and the whole community that there was always surveillance taking place.

Cheering erupted from the back room when Big Doug left the building..

Big Doug and Owyhee Kenny were long-time friends.

They had raised their children together.

They had gone on farming trips together.

They had helped each other.

There wasn't any judgment for Big Doug, just sadness.

As Owyhee Kenny was sitting, waiting, the cheering continued, like a bass drum pounding.

He nervously picked up the single book and read the author bio.

Brian Mittge grew up in Lewis County, on a farm. His closest friend was a bunny named "Rabbi McFunbunns". Brian took his schooling very seriously. His interest in George Washington of Centralia started when he, in a school assignment on

presidents, accidentally used the wrong
George Washington."

The distraction didn't help. The cheering coupled
with his long-time friendship with Big Doug
increased Owyhee Kenny's resolve to hold onto
his potato farm for as long as he could.

He was called back to the conference
room. It was the same conference room and the
same cast of characters as every other year,
however, something was clearly different.

Each year, the waiting room got emptier
and emptier. Owyhee Kenny knew that he had to
up his game this year. Every year, the meeting
with the SIPC was important, but this year, it
was epicly monumental.

Sparky was waiting in the conference
room. When Owyhee Kenny got there, Sparky
sprung to his feet, extended his hand and said,
"Hello Owyhee Kenny, welcome back! We have
known each other a long time. I am glad you
could make it. Can I get you a Betta? or water?
Have you been able to get all of the mashed
potatoes out of everywhere?"

The two men had known each other for a
lifetime. In fact, Sparky had even helped Owyhee
Kenny originate his nickname.

***

In the fourth grade, Owyhee Kenny wrote
a report on the neighboring Owyhee Mountains.
His report didn't focus on the vast natural
beauty, the lush wildlife, the seasonal
landscapes, or the very ironic fact that Owyhee

15

Mountains were named after the archipelago of Hawaii because of their similarities.

His chosen report topic was the Owyhee Dwarves, a race of cannibalistic, cave-dwelling, two-foot tall, naked little-people with tails, that kidnap children and eat them.

It was not on the list of suggested topics.

To make matters worse, it was an oral presentation. Other children were finishing their report on the Philadelphus Lewisii, the state flower.

Young Kenny got up to give the most remarkable presentation on the Owyhee Dwarves that Southeast Idaho had ever seen. The report was complete with maps and hand-drawn illustrations of the dwarves eating children. His crayon box was now one red crayon short of a set.

Kenny was proud of his report and believed that it was sincerely the best report written or presented, ever.

He started the presentation with the line "Do you think that a race of two-foot tall, cannibalistic, naked, cave-dwelling dwarves could carry a dead elk on their backs? Well, I am here to tell you that they can. A male elk can weigh up to 700 lbs. Which makes it all the more remarkable that a two-foot tall dwarf would be capable of such a feat. Numerous first-hand accounts have been reported with eye-witness sightings all documented here on this map. They are also the sworn protectors of water."

He went on to describe the other possible uses of the dwarf tails or the evolutionary benefit of growing tails in the first place. He shared maps and caves and how those possible habitats would benefit the little people. The class, wide-eyed, was mesmerized and silent. When Kenny completed his presentation, there was no applause. No hands shot up with questions. His teacher just said, "Well, that will be our last report of the day." She then poured something into her coffee and announced: "we are going to play Heads-up-7-up for the remaining 1.5 hours of the scheduled time for class presentations."

It was at recess that Sparky and his friends Sparky and Hubba approached young Kenny and suggested that he would be known as "Owyhee Kenny, the hero of dwarves." The nickname stuck, or just Owyhee Kenny for short.

***

That was a long time ago. Presently, there are two men discussing the future of potato farming in Blackfoot. Owyhee Kenny's arm met Sparky's arm half-way across the table. The hand came with such velocity that it felt like a viper striking its prey. Sparky's hand matched with a python grip.

Sparky was a bad dude. This was a game for him. A game that he was planning on winning. Winning was a drug, and he felt special delight in this victory. Owyhee Kenny was his foe today. The room now was oozing with testosterone and pressure. It was dog eat dog in that room and Owyhee Kenny was wearing milk bone underwear. He knew it.

17

PRO TIP: According to Chinese astrology, dogs and snakes get along well. There is a 75% chance of compatibility.

The two men sat down at the table. Now, a game of high-stakes poker but there were no cards and the dealer had left the room. The big chip stack was sitting in front of Sparky, and Owyhee Kenny was being asked to call with a bad hand, pocket "2"s.

Sparky slowly raised himself from his chair without his gaze ever straying from the eyes of Owyhee Kenny. He placed his hands on either side of the table, where he introduced a pregnant pause. A pause that started uncomfortably and had no end in sight. It was so quiet you could hear the hands of the askew clock in the lobby ticking.

Sparky looked at Owyhee Kenny, Owyhee Kenny looked back at Sparky, each studying the other. The features, the wrinkles earned through hard work, the glances, they were looking for a gesture that could give one the advantage over the other. Neither man flinched.

At long last, Sparky took a deep breath.

The breath destroyed the pause, breaking the air. Now, there was a lot of breathing and a lot of pausing. These two men were engaged in an old-fashioned breathing standoff. Breathing, pausing, pausing, breathing.

Finally, Sparky cleared his throat and said, "Owyhee Kenny, we want your farm, we have a very nice package for you." And Sparky slid the blue folder across the table.

As the blue folder came into his reach, he slowly opened the folder and looked down. The offer looked different from previous years. In this case, Owyhee Kenny knew that different meant bad.

Every year, he showed up. He played nice and looked at the offer. Then, he would pause for 30 seconds, breathe out loud and then offer up some excuse as to why he just couldn't sell this year.

"We just planted a new variety of potato."

"Dorothea is pregnant and needs to have the baby on the farm,"

"We are hosting a live theater performance of "Shakespeare's Othello."

It couldn't be about money, it had to be about passion for potatoes.

This year was different, Owyhee Kenny looked up and to the right as though he was pondering the weight of the offer. Everything was on the line and he had to keep all of his "poker tells" close. He had no intention of accepting the offer but had to appear as though he was really considering this one. At long last, his eyes drifted back over to Sparky and with eye contact, he murmured in a voice just loud enough to be heard, "Sparky, this is a very attractive offer, you know that I will need to consult my attorney on the matter."

Sparky, a seasoned negotiator didn't think that he had won. He believed that Owyhee Kenny was on the ropes.

"Of course you will, you have 72 hours,

don't delay though as we are planning our next two-quarters, and our top priority is setting the price of the potato. Side note, you may want to check your water quality, I hear something weird is going around." This was no veiled threat. It was very clear.

Big Potato had locked up all of the farms in town. They had also locked up everything, attorneys, accountants, elected officials. A person could not so much as sneeze in this town without Big Potato knowing it.

Owyhee Kenny didn't have an attorney, nor did he plan to find one.

With great composure, he picked up the blue folder, tucked it under his left arm and grinned. He extended his right hand to Sparky. The two men shook hands and Owyhee Kenny promptly exited.

Chompers, still faithfully waiting, followed Owyhee Kenny as he walked directly out to his blue truck and got in. He clutched the keys and slowly turned the engine on. He drove the truck just two blocks until he was just out of view of the office park. He pulled the truck over. He turned the engine off. He leaned his head against the steering wheel, and began to cry. He cried, and cried and cried because he knew this year, he would have to take the offer. He was behind on mortgage payments, was out of money, and didn't have a plan.

As Owyhee Kenny left the SIPC, Sparky ran back to his office to watch Owyhee Kenny leave the building and get into his blue pickup truck. Sparky had wired the whole town for surveillance. The sign in the lobby of the SIPC that read, "The eyes of the potato are watching you," was telling the truth. The only footage of Sparky destroying the potato festival was owned by the SIPC. Sparky had already collected it and added it to his trophy case of evil.

Today, the eyes of the potato were watching Owyhee Kenny. Sparky watched him pull his truck over and cry. He took great pleasure in watching a once-proud man soak his blue pickup truck in tears.

Sparky watched Owyhee Kenny start his truck back up. He also watched him drive the farm roads back to the potato farm where Owyhee Kenny lived to see his lovely wife Dorothea and discover what had been done to his greatest asset, the water.

Check the Water

Spirit water is water imbued
with spiritual energy, providing it with
special healing properties. It is often taken
from sources where spiritual energy is
considered to be particularly strong.
- Hippy, The Internet

The "Check the water," comment that Sparky
made had Owyhee Kenny very nervous. He had
the best water in the state. It was the key to the
success of his potatoes. Owyhee Kenny also had
fear about the possibility of losing his potato
farm. He had fear about losing all that he had
built, part of which was the water filter.

When Owyhee Kenny met and married his
wife Dorothea, they purchased a plot of land.
They dragged a trailer to the property to set up
their own homestead. Day-by-day, they built a
house on site while growing potatoes.

This is the origin of Owyhee Kenny's

potato farm. It started with a piece of property that nobody wanted. He borrowed money from family to buy a rocky and barren lot. The property was a wreck. It's one shining feature was natural, water rights from the Snake River.

Envision the Snake River, meandering around large chunks of rock, jettisoning out of the earth. The water teeming with life, sportsman catching large fish from the shore while white water rafters drift by. In the distance, mama elk and her babes drinking from the source. This river was *life*.

 GET TO KNOW IDAHO: In 1965, Evel Knievel drew special attention to Idaho in his failed attempt to jump the mile-wide chasm on a motorcycle that is the Snake River.

This was not the situation for Dorothea's family. The Ibaigurens had an irrigation ditch that filled a reservoir on their property. It was dirty. It was dank. It was theirs.

Dorothea's father was a water-purification engineer. He was brilliant, but was so focused on water quality that he was absent from every other area of his life. Her lonely mother self-medicated with drugs and alcohol. She wasn't dangerous. She was empty and hollow.

Because she raised herself, Dorothea was quite unique.

She spoke British-English. She had never been to England, but during her early years, much of her time was spent watching BBC on the telly. When she went away to kindergarten, she realized that she spoke British-English. Dorothea liked the attention though, so she kept it up.

Dorothea graduated from Spirit Lake High School in Northern Idaho.

Immediately following High School, Owyhee Kenny and Dorothea got married. Dorothea's parents built and installed a water purification system for the farm. It wasn't just any purification system, though. It was the best that a world-class water purification engineer could create.

Dorothea's father was the best that there was. He received international acclaim for his work on clean water in Spirit Lake, Idaho.

Other couples receive bone china or something off their registry. Owyhee Kenny and Dorothea received something far more valuable. Something that would help them over and over again, clean water. It was that water that made their potatoes so good. It was also the water that enabled Dorothea to have her own garden to help through the lean times.

She was thrifty. She had to be. She milled her own flour and yeast and stored it in the basement.

The threat of Sparky and his goons doing something to the water supply was pretty unnerving. Big Potato had a bunch of heavies that offered "protection" and "enforcement." The heavies were known as the Potato Heads. In an unfortunately predictable manner, the leader of the Potato Heads was called Mr. Potato Head. (his name was actually Hubba.) He was the same person that co-named Owyhee Kenny so many years ago.

Owyhee Kenny got home. He immediately ran to the filtration system. At first pass, everything looked the same. He got down on his hands and knees and inspected every aspect of the circulation. He tasted the water at every stage in the cleansing.

When you have something as valuable as the filtration system, you secure it. It was locked and showed no signs of being tampered with. However, Owyhee Kenny was visibly shaken.

Having to check the filtration system allowed Owyhee Kenny to focus on fixing something, instead of worrying about the imminent threat of losing his farm.

Owyhee Kenny was exhausted. He slinked back into the house where the armchair enveloped him.

Dorothea knew her husband, and she could tell something was wrong without him even speaking. So she sat down, looked him in the eyes and said, "What's got your knickers in a twist? How was your meeting with Big Potato?"

Owyhee Kenny was not a strong communicator, and he was handicapped with the potential loss of the water supply and farm still on his mind. But, as a good husband, he attempted a reply, "It was rough. Sparky said something about checking the water."

"Knees up chum! What does that mean?" she inquired.

"I don't know," he said. There was a long pause.

"Sounds like they are playing dingy. Is there anything rotten with the water?" She said.

Owyhee Kenny was still thinking through everything when he said, "I don't know, I have checked everything, it doesn't look like anything has been touched. But, the fact that he brought up the water means that they are thinking about it. If they damage our water supply, no amount of money will be able to save our farm."

Dorothea grabbed Owyhee Kenny by both hands, pulled him forward and said, "We are strong! This is our farm; we built it. We built this house. Nobody is going to take it from us. If they try, we are going to have an old-fashioned argy-bargy."

Dorothea was known for being a bit of a firecracker, and sometimes incomprehensible. Owyhee Kenny had all kinds of questions about what his wife meant but was unable to process anything else at the time. So he appreciated the sentiment and the effort and moved on.

She, on the other hand, was calculating much more nefarious intentions. Mama bears do that.

This is the most challenging situation that they had ever faced in their lives.

This was real.

This was their past.

This was their present.

This was their future.

And it was all hanging in the balance.

Sparky

Villains Gotta Vill

James 3:3-5

3 When we put bits into the mouths of horses to make them obey us, we can turn the whole animal. 4 Or take ships as an example. Although they are so large and are driven by strong winds, they are steered by a very small rudder wherever the pilot wants to go. 5 Likewise, the tongue is a small part of the body, but it makes great boasts. Consider what a great forest is set on fire by a small spark.
- Bible, New International Version

Hubba was at his stand-up desk. The doctor has suggested, for his posture, to stand instead of sitting.

Sparky materialized from nothing and said, "I have an idea. Let's head down to the school, and squeeze the kid. I can't remember the last time we leaned on someone together. Remember the good ol' days?"

Hubba replied, "It has been a long time. I don't know Sparky, my head is just not in the game any more. I'll go, but I can't guarantee that it will be my best work."

Like a child dressed in Sunday best, forced to go to church, Sparky and Hubba visited the local High School. The same school where Owyhee Kenny's son, Russ, was a student.

Unexpectedly, Sparky was taken aback with emotion as he walked into this place. He had attended Blackfoot High School so many years ago.

Sparky's high school memories were not filled with high school football games and prom. Instead, they were cold and dark.

His parents had attempted and failed to start a sweet potato farm. It took a toll. It left emptiness and poverty in its wake.

After that experience, Sparky's only extracurricular activity was the SIPC. His job was to make bank deposits each month from member dues.

Both men were weighed down with memories, albeit vastly different ones. They shared a single goal, rattling the cage of young Russ Ibaiguren.

Sparky knew that he could push on Owyhee Kenny as much as he could muster and the man would probably still weather the attack.

29

However, if he could get to the boy or the wife, then Sparky knew he could probably get the farm.

Hubba and Sparky authoritatively walked into the school and passed the guidance counselor's office on the way to the main office. And what to their surprise was taking place, a meeting between Russ, and his Guidance Counselor, Ms. Yamada.

Russ was a smart kid, but sometimes relationships with other people were sometimes difficult.

He was crazy-smart.

He was a science kid always doing experiments, mixing chemicals and lighting things on fire. It was his way.

He was not eloquent.

He was not articulate.

He was curious.

It was more of a sign of immaturity than a disorder. That was why he was in the guidance counselor's office.

Russ was a good kid. His science obsession was the primary reason that he would ever get into trouble. And although an annoyance to the teaching staff at Blackfoot High School, he was welcomed by the administration. His teachers would say that he got "lost" in his own brain. This is why he was always sent to the guidance counselor. His misbehavior did not warrant discipline, just space.

Hubba and Sparky had just "won" the lottery. Russ was sitting there, with his guidance counselor. Her name was Christa Yamada. Her family moved to Idaho in the 1940s when 110,000 Japanese-Americans were moved to internment camps to protect the rest of the country from legal Japanese-American citizens.

Ms. Yamada's family was originally from Bainbridge Island in Washington State. They were one of the first families forced to relocate during World War II. They moved to Blackfoot, Idaho.

The ironic part of the move was that Ms. Yamada's family enjoyed Idaho. They liked the weather, the heat in the summer and the cold in the winter. The Gem State, Idaho suited them well, so they stayed.

Russ stumbled into her office 3-4 times per week and each time Russ would be just escaping from his own world. Ms. Yamada loved Russ. She was a good educator, and a good person. Shet became an educator because she wanted to help people learn. Every time Russ came, Ms. Yamada would just say "Russ, I see you are here again in my office, is everything okay?"

To which Russ would reply, "We sure do have a lot of clocks in this school" or "why is our mascot the bronco?"

Ms. Yamada wanted better for Russ. She knew that punishment was not the answer, as Russ wasn't doing anything wrong. He was just being himself. Ms. Yamada had to engage Russ on a human level and always looked for how to do that well.

Earlier that morning, Ms. Yamada had said, "Hey Russ, how about we make a clock, out of potatoes." Russ thought for a long moment as if he were a code talker in World War II deciphering the Hopi language. He grinned from ear to ear, his joy was electric and thought that this was a fantastic idea.

 PRO TIP: When making a potato clock, two potatoes is enough, more is excessive.

Hubba and Sparky looked on, puzzled as Ms. Yamada and Russ went on to unpack the supplies. There were 213 potatoes in all. Ms. Yamada said, "This ought to be enough," and she studied each potato as though it were a family heirloom or a gift. The situation was a "7" on the awkward scale, but so was Russ, so it fit.

Ms. Yamada stood up, grabbed her keys and winked at Russ and said, "I'll go raid the science supplies!"

Sparky said, "Hello, Russ, my name is Sparky, I work with the Southeast Idaho Potato Council. I know your dad. Has he talked to you about what is going on with your farm?"

Russ sat there, unresponsive.

A villain has got to vill so Sparky continued, "That's OK, you don't have to answer. I came to the high school today to talk to you. You and I actually have a lot in common. My parents moved here from the former Soviet Union. They had a brief stop in Nashville, North Carolina. Nashville happens to be the largest sweet potato producing place in the United States. They wanted a better life and they wanted to accomplish that by growing sweet potatoes here in Idaho. No one was interested. It bankrupted them. After that, I never once saw any life behind my father's eyes. He died a pauper's death without a cent to his name. He doesn't even have a gravestone. This is where you come in, after meeting with your dad the other day, I was worried that he might be going down the same path that my father went down. Because of that, I offered to buy your farm. I even offered more money than it was worth in the case that he had some other financial issues. No one should have to go through what I went through."

 PRO TIP: North Carolina and Tennessee share a border, and a town called Nashville.

Russ sat silent.

Sparky continued, "This is Hubba, he saw it all too, my family came and lived at his family's farm. You know if you ever need anything, I will help, and I will bring the full power of the SIPC with me."

Russ knew enough about Sparky and the SIPC. He knew that these words were empty and manipulative.

It was at this point that Ms. Yamada returned with science supplies on a "rolley" cart.

Russ was visibly shaken, but he started to look at the contents on the cart and quickly snapped out of his fog.

Sparky and Hubba were still looking for opportunities to extend their visit with Russ, so they stayed and helped make potato clocks.

The two men, Russ, and his guidance counselor went on to make 106 potato clocks. There was just one potato leftover. You see that it took two potatoes to power a single clock.

This day was confusing for Russ. He loved science, but Sparky and Hubba, ever present, were discombobulating.

Each clock required two potatoes, where two zinc rods were jammed into the side of both potatoes, connected with wires and then connected to a digital clock. A potato battery is what is called an electrochemical battery. The zinc in the nail reacts with the copper wire and the acidity of the potato to create electricity. That electricity is used to power the clock.

Russ jammed the zinc rods into the side of the potatoes and Ms. Yamada was in charge of wrapping the copper wire around each nail.

Their assembly line was much more efficient than the individual effort of Hubba and Sparky.

106 clocks took the entire afternoon. Ms. Yamada planned 15 minutes into her day for the making of a potato clock. She knew that it was important, so she made more time. Good people do that.

After all the clocks were made, there was one potato left. The end of making the potato clocks was the beginning of something much more calculated.

Ms. Yamada and Russ immediately left the room with their clocks. As they left, Sparky offered one last barb, "You have a beautiful family, I wouldn't want anything to happen to it."

Russ and Ms. Yamada kept walking.

When no one was looking, Sparky grabbed the last potato and in a single motion of his hand slammed it on the table into what seemed to be a 100 small pieces.

Hubba on the other hand, saved one of the clocks for himself that he was particularly proud of.

Both as a response to two very strange men in her office, and the fact that she and Russ had just finished a very large number of potato clocks, Ms. Yamada thought that this moment might be an excellent time for a little positive PR. She suggested that they take the clocks to the local nursing home. They would share a clock with each of the guests. Russ thought that this was a great idea, so the two of them hopped in Ms. Yamada's Chevy Celebrity. They drove with 105 potato clocks to the local nursing home.

The two of them walked room by room delivering clocks. Each guest had different cognitive abilities. Some of them were fully functional, very responsive and excited for the company. Others were just excited about human contact. All of the guests had a new potato clock that would tell time until the potatoes rolled.

It was 9:45 p.m. at night and Russ and Ms. Yamada had finally finished the clock distribution. They were both tired. The length of the day showed on their faces. It was a long day, but it was a good day. They both fell into the Chevy Celebrity, drove to Russs's house and called it a night. As the two pulled up to Russ's house there was a car parked across the street that neither person had seen before. Inside the car was none other than the man that had visited Russ at School that afternoon. It was Hubba and the glowing embers of a burning cigarette.

She Punched Back

Let your plans be dark and impenetrable as night, and when you move, fall like a thunderbolt.

- **Sun Tzu**, *The Art of War*

Russ walked into the house and his mother, Dorothea was still up, milling about. She asked how his day was. He could not stop talking about it. He loved making the clocks out of the potatoes. At some point, he shared just how many clocks he made, and Dorothea started to laugh uncontrollably.

"You are an amazing, creative young man. You never fail to surprise me," she said.

After the laughter stopped, Russ went on, "There was something else, some men showed up to my school today. I knew of them but didn't know them, but they knew me, I think that there were from the potato council. It was really weird."

Dorothea glanced out the window and saw the car parked outside. She had had enough. She was ready to punch back. She picked up the phone and dialed 9-1-1. The voice on the other end of the phone picked up and said, "Hello, 9-1-1, what is your emergency"

"Yes, Allo, this is Dorothea Ibaiguren, there is a strange car parked across the street from my house," she said.

"Hi Dorothea, it is not uncommon for cars to be parked places, would you like us to dispatch a police car?" said the 9-1-1 operator.

She responded, "Well, you could, but the thing is, I have never seen this car before, and, I know this will sound crazy, but I have reason to believe that there might be a bomb inside the car."

She didn't believe there was a bomb inside the car. However, she knew that the BPD had recently acquired a tank and they really wanted to use it.

Everyone in town knew that the police department had received a tank as part of a program that the federal government. There was surplus inventory and the tank was awarded to the city as part of an anti-terrorism grant. The city wanted to prepare in that case that a terrorist bomb would find its way to rural, central Idaho.

That meant that there was a tank in the motor pool. It also meant that the Blackfoot

Police Department really, really, really wanted to put it into action.

The BPD didn't know that Hubba was across was watching the Ibaigurens, so even though the department was owned by the SIPC, they were going to respond.

She was going to get the tank deployed to address the potato head situation across the street.

The 9-1-1 operator responded, "please hold while I put you in touch with the bomb control unit."

With a couple of click noises, another voice picked up amidst the sounds of pins falling at the local bowling alley an excited voice rang out, "Hello, <pins falling> this is the Blackfoot Bomb Control unit, how can I help you?<pins falling>" It was clear that the call had been forwarded to an officer who was off-duty.

"Lovely, yes this is Dorothea Ibaiguren and I am concerned that there is a strange car parked across the street. I have a strong belief that there might just be a bomb inside the car," she said.

The officer also knew that there was not a bomb. That said any phone call about a bomb in the community was enough of a reason to leave league night to fire up the tank, and spring to action.

Dorothea smiled and hung up the phone.

Russ looked at her and said, "what did you just do?"

She replied, "I just punched back. The bobbies will be here with a tank cannon pointed at the driver's side window within the hour."

Dorothea put a pot of water on for tea.
She waited.
She made tea.
She made English biscuits.
Russ waited.
They drank tea.
They ate English biscuits.

Dorothea was fierce, she loved her family deeply and would do anything for them. She knew that the life that she had created for her family was eroding. She also knew that she would not go down swinging. She would fight for what she had, and she would fight to keep it.

Forty-five minutes later, a low rumble, gradually growing in intensity, echoed down the street. Yes, the tank was rumbling down the road, in response to the bomb scare.

As the tank got closer, it got louder and louder. When it pulled up alongside Hubba's late-model sports car, it was in full bomb-detection mode.

The turret slowly spun until the barrel was pointing directly at Hubba's head on the driver's side.

Only the glass from his window and about 6 inches were separating him from the barrel of his impending doom. He was torn between peeing himself and pleading for his life.

He began to plead.

The sounds coming out of the late model sports car were enough to cause the tank operator to unscrew the hatch and pop his head out.

"Do you have a bomb in this car?" the tank operator shouted.

Hubba shouted back, "No, I don't have a bomb, I don't have anything. Please don't shoot me with your extremely large tank, please don't shoot me. I don't have a bomb. I have these breath mints. I have mail, looks like a jury summons," holding up a stack of mail that was in his passenger seat. He continued, "BUT, I do not have a bomb!"

The tank operator grumbled, "too bad."

He closed the hatch, screwed it tight, fired up the tank and drove back to the police station where the tank would sit only firing up for community outreach events.

Hubba, clearly shaken, turned his car on, and proceeded to drive home where he laid awake all night processing what had just happened. He reflected on whether working with the SIPC was what he still wanted to do.

Near-death experiences brought by tanks will do that.

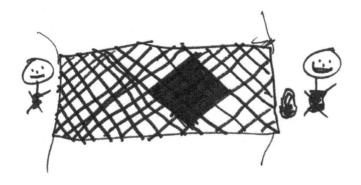

Large Teeth,
but Tiny Arms

*"Yes, we'll win this game, the old-fashioned
way, the tried and true way: we'll cheat!"*
                                    - *Skeletor*

In retaliation to the tank scare, the Potato Heads
showed up again to visit Russ. There were two,
both under the age of thirty. They took their jobs
with the SIPC after High School. Always
intending to get a better job, but it never
happened. Now their life was relegated to
harassing a young man. They followed Russ
home. He was walking, they were driving an
uncomfortably slow pickup. Finally, Russ, a bit
agitated, turned around and snipped, "Why are
you following me?"

The Potato Heads, taken aback,
responded, "Hey Russ, how are you?" They kept
driving and Russ didn't respond. This silent
treatment became a bit of a challenge for the
Potato Heads.

"Aren't you going to answer, this is petty,

what kind of parents do you have that you wouldn't even answer an adult when you are addressed directly?" His response was a stone-cold stare and a lack of response.

They continued, "So that's how it is going to be, fine we can talk, you don't have to. Look, we saw some folks prowling around your farm last night and we were concerned. We waited to make sure that you and your mom and dad were all okay. We are probably going to just take extra care to make sure you guys are okay."

Finally, Russ could handle it no longer and finally lashed out and said "Look, I know what you guys are doing. You are trying to scare us. You can't do it. You are parasites. The only reason that you exist is to hassle people like us. Well, guess what, we are the last farm. You won't have a job anymore when you have scared everyone away, and then you will be no different than us. I hope you don't get sick or need your car fixed because no one will help you. You arc people used for corporate profit and as soon as you are no longer needed, you are discarded. You are dinosaurs, with have large teeth, but tiny arms. Newsflash, Dinosaurs are extinct."

The potato heads were blown away by the articulate young man and his venomous response. They began to slow clap. "Wow, he talks, and kitty has claws. Listen we don't want any trouble, we just want to make sure that your family is safe, we all want the same things."

A quick curt response from Russ, "If you want to help, then leave us alone."

Strong Armory

*When people hurt you over and over, think of
them like sandpaper; They may scratch and
hurt you a bit, but in the end, you end up
polished and they end up useless.*
                                      - Chris Colfer

After messing with Russ, the Potato Heads were
headed to an all-hands meeting

Hubba was early, preparing for his weekly
team meeting with the potato heads. This was
originally organized and run by none other than
the top potato himself, Sparky. Initially, he
would attend every meeting of the potato heads,
but as the SIPC grew, his attendance
diminished.

The potato heads were an interesting
bunch. They were a blend of industry henchmen
with a penchant for strong-armory. They were
true innovators of the intimidation trade.

46

Although they did like to apply pressure to the downtrodden potato farmer, they liked to have a certain panache about it. They wanted a clear connection between the creator and the product.

Sparky hired Hubba, and Hubba hired his team. The stated purpose of the team was to provide security for local potato farmers. When the potato heads were first formed, they would do things like leave dead animals on the porches of potato farmers. They wanted to create that immediate fear that something is wrong. It was a bit cliché. The spectacle was the kind of thing that you might see on a Friday night, made for cable movie. For most of the potato heads, this kind of gesture felt empty. Yes, they wanted to scare the pants off of the farmer, but they needed a level of originality to keep their own interest.

When you combine bored young men with Attention Deficit Disorder, you get nothing short of spectacular results. Admiring the byproduct of this group is a bit akin to admiring the torture techniques used to elicit information in from prisoners of war during the Vietnam conflict. But, if you can forget that their shenanigans were created and intended for the sheer purpose of ruining someone's life, you can appreciate the level of depth that the potato heads would take on.

The sophistication of the spectacle grew with each incident.

 PRO TIP: If you like your job, you never have to work a day in your life.

One incident included a temporary laser light show that cast moons and stars on to the neighboring hillside with a message that said, "Leave now or..." The periods kept repeating and dancing around the hillside. The potato heads sat in the car with the radio listening to the William Tell Overture. The lights painted images on the adjacent hillside. The song drew to an end with the culminating message painted on the hillside in laser light "no one will". It was a bit confusing for the potato farmers, but it was an epic build up to the climax of the message. In spite of the misappropriated spectacle, the farmers seem to always understand that they were no longer welcome.

Then, there was the enormous vat of Jello carefully constructed with layers of color suspending potatoes inside of the Jello and message in clear gelatin appearing to float four feet off of the ground as the Robert Frost poem "October," with just a few modifications.

> For the ~~grapes~~ **potatoes'** *sake, if they were all,*
> Whose ~~leaves~~ **roots** *already are burnt with frost,*
> Whose clustered fruit must else be lost—
> For the ~~grapes~~ **potatoes'** *sake along the* ~~wall~~ **fail.**

Even though replacing the word potato with grape seems trivial, for the potato heads, this was a victory in the ability to bring some high class to the intimidation game.

The Potato Heads were increasing the pressure on the community. It was air/ground attack. The Potato Heads would apply constant pressure and Sparky would swoop in and finish things off. And this approach had worked on every farm in town, with just one exception.

The Potato heads parked outside the farmer's house, schools, church. They would follow them through the grocery store. The purpose was to make sure that the farmer ALWAYS knew that they were being watched. Strange things would happen to the farmer as well. Unexplainable things. Things would break that should have never broken. The problem is that the potato heads were good, you could never, ever find evidence that they had been involved.

While planning for the Ibairguren intimidation, one of the Potato Heads began to speak up and was immediately cut off. "I swear to the Great God in Heaven that if you are going to suggest again that we build a roller coaster and amusement park and pretend like it is haunted to lure in an unsuspecting group of teenagers and a talking dog as the big reveal, I will make it my life's purpose to ruin your current relationships, your future relationships, and your past relationships."

The same potato head replied, "First off, you can't ruin past relationships unless you were to build a time machine..."

To which he was immediately cut off with "We are not going to build a time machine to go back in time and scare Owyhee Kenny out of running the potato farm in the first place.

Owyhee Kenny wouldn't exist and then he couldn't even own the farm. All of our effort to scare him away would be lost."

Then a loud voice boomed in from Mr. Potato Head, "Gentlemen, I have this idea. We make a dinosaur, big mouth, short arms" Gears started to turn, eyes lit up;

"One of the potato heads, to claim the idea as his own, asked the question "What if we were to make a t-rex?" It was settled the king of all dinosaurs would be erected on the homestead to scare the family away.

So, for the week that followed, the potato heads had been going by wrecking yards, garage sales, scrap heaps, everything. They were collecting metal parts so that they could weld a near scale size Tyrannosaurus Rex. The composition was that the T-Rex would be flattening potatoes under its feet. There would be potatoes held in its squatty little arms and there would be potato parts hanging out of its mouth. It was important that in the effort to communicate the rather non-trivial message of "get out, leave, sell the farm," each potato was hand-painted to look like one of the Ibaigurens. A scale model of the farm was placed under the foot of the rather large metal dinosaur.

***

Days passed, and turned into weeks. The pressure was working, Owyhee Kenny felt It. After receiving the offer on the farm, he couldn't sleep. The clock was ticking and he knew he had to do something. He knew what was coming from the SIPC and more specifically the potato heads. He knew that he couldn't afford a fight, and he knew that he believed that he was out of options.

In Blackfoot, you always knew who the target of the SIPC was because the potato heads were hassling them. So when the Ibaigurens started to receive special attention from the potato heads, Dorothea knew something was up. She asked, "Why are the Potato Heads following me around?"

Owyhee Kenny responded, "You know they are trying to buy the farm, they do this every year."

After some pause, Dorothea continued, "I know, but this year it is different, it is like they are more aggressive."

Owyhee Kenny attempted to calm his wife, he grabbed her, hugged her and whispered, "This will pass, it always does. They will hassle us for a couple of days and then move to other things."

She protested, "I don't like this, Kenny, I'm upside down about our safety."

Owyhee Kenny straightened up and said very boldly, "This is what they do, they are dogs on a leash, they aren't going to do anything." Dorothea responded, "They have done things to other people, people we know, people we used to farm with. You know they weren't that different than us. They didn't do anything wrong."

In a final effort to comfort his wife, Owyhee Kenny looked her square in the eye and said, "Listen, I know this is scary right now, but we have to believe that this is going to be okay."

Owyhee Kenny knew that he couldn't say

"No" to Big Potato this time. The train had not only left the station. It was pulling into its destination. As Owyhee Kenny considered the calculus of the situation, he knew that all paths led through Big Potato. He was pinched. There was pressure on all sides.

Diamonds are formed when pressure is applied to carbon. Carbon is everywhere, and so is pressure. So what causes diamonds to be formed in some cases and not in others? It has everything to do with the amount of pressure. The conditions required to convert carbon matter into a diamond are so intense, there is no other place for the carbon to go but for a chemical reaction that transforms it from ordinary materials into extraordinary diamonds.

Owyhee Kenny was facing that kind of pressure. It was coming in on all sides. His son, his wife, his farm, his way of life. Glancing at Chompers brought relief because he just loved him and expected nothing in return.

It was 11 o'clock at night when all of a sudden there was a knock at the door. It was one of the potato heads. The man stood in the doorway, rain falling all around him and said, "I just wanted to check in on you just to make sure that everything was okay."

Owyhee Kenny responded, "Everything is fine, you know we don't need you here."

To which the man replied, "I just noticed that your lights were on and wanted to make sure everything was okay."

Again Owyhee Kenny replied, "Everything is okay, I am going to ask you to leave now." See, Owyhee Kenny would have called the police but knew that the potato heads were in cahoots with the local police department.

The man said "Listen, I just want to make sure that your family is okay. Don't get mad at me."

The man went back to the car, where glowing embers immediately relit. This only lasted for a few minutes as he was just waiting for the lights in the house to go out because once the lights were out, the magic begins.

Because this may be the last time that the Potato Heads would be able to apply pressure to the potato farmers, they wanted to do it right. It had to be the single greatest convergence between pressure and artistic expression.

The potato heads were remarkably quiet in assembling this masterpiece. All of the weldings had been done in the shop earlier that week. At this point, the assembly of the figure was more like putting together a snap-tight model. There was one point in the night where there was a commotion and the potato heads thought that they had been found out, but the noise had come from Satan's spawn, a lonely raccoon.

The next morning when Owyhee Kenny woke up, he opened the door to see a rather large, 14-feet tall, metal dinosaur standing on a scale model of his farm while he and his family were being impaled. Had the situation been different, the response would have been awe, as the dinosaur was quite magnificent.

Pieces of the Blackfoot history were interwoven to form the shape of the coelurosaurian theropod. The head, body, arms, claws were formed by welding the lid of a BBQ a lawnmower, dishwasher, bike chains, car axle, bicycles, chicken wire, hot water heater saw blades and other pieces of metal discarded by the Blackfoot community. The item used to intimidate this family was assembled from pieces central to Blackfoot families. Items discarded when they were no longer of use.

The final product was truly a sight to behold and nothing short of spectacular.

At daybreak, when Owyhee Kenny awoke, he noticed the new visitor on the porch. He took a deep breath, leaned against the doorframe and sank into the weight of his situation. After about five minutes Owyhee Kenny went back into the kitchen to fix himself a delicious sandwich and a vodka tonic even though it was still quite early in the day.

At this point in time, for Owyhee Kenny, he hoped that he might just be able to postpone the inevitable. He was sitting on the family's large overstuffed chair nursing a drink. He was rubbing the cap of a vodka bottle. He was drinking his sorrow away, and then he had an idea. With each rub of the bottle cap, the idea became more and more clear.

Owyhee Kenny couldn't stop big potato, but he might be able to postpone him losing his potato farm, to maintain their life for a little bit longer.

Inspiration comes serendipitously, Owyhee Kenny studied the t-rex and as he was admiring the monstrosity, he pondered, "If he could stage an accident that would buy him some time," and time might be just what he needed. It needed to be believable and large enough to command the delay of selling the farm, AND it had to be real. He knew that he couldn't tell anyone but Chompers, not Dorothea, not Russ, not anyone, not ever.

Owyhee Kenny stood up, patted Chompers on the head and walked over to the key rack. Hanging just next to the door, a key ring with a single yellow fishing float and from it hung a key. He grabbed it, walked outside, climbed in the family tractor lovingly nicknamed Ridey McTractor and, with the turn of the key, started a plan that would alter their lives forever.

Ridey McTractor

Examine each question in terms of what is ethically and aesthetically right, as well as what is economically expedient. A thing is right when it tends to preserve the integrity, stability, and beauty of the biotic community. It is wrong when it tends otherwise.

— Aldo Leopold

Lots of people name their cars. Some people name their ping pong paddle. The Ibaigurens named their tractor. It was an old tractor, but it was part of the family and as such, she had a name. The family tractor's name was Ridey McTractor. Russ named the tractor when he was a wee lad. It was his way of asking for a ride on the tractor, and it stuck as a name.

Owyhee Kenny was poised atop Ridey

McTractor, a machine that had served their family for so long. It was originally purchased new, but handed down by Owyhee Kenny's father. It had been repaired more times than you can count. The only original thing left of the tractor was the chassis. Parts were traded, back and forth. When you absolutely couldn't trade for parts, there was a man out of Meridian, Idaho where you could get the part that you need. Sometimes he could pay with a trade like "pumpernickel," sometimes he had to pay with cash. Either way, Ridey McTractor was always in fine working order.

Owyhee Kenny was a confused man. He loved his wife, his son, his family. Ultimately he loved his life. However, life as he knew it was about to change. He hadn't shared much about his meeting with Dorothea, although she "knew" everything.

In all of his years of marriage to Dorothea, Owyhee Kenny had never lied to her. He was the picture of integrity. His plan, and not telling Dorothea about it was out of character.

These decisions cannot be made without internal emotional consequences and Owyhee Kenny knew this. That is why he sat in his chair for so long contemplating. He gingerly moved to the door. He was a man divided between protecting the life of his family and the life that he has always known and his own character.

Owyhee Kenny had nothing left. His mental faculties were a bowl of mashed potatoes. He was so overwhelmed that he couldn't think straight. Somewhere deep inside of him, he had this idea that he could save the farm. He would stage a dramatic accident. At least he could buy some time. Though it wouldn't make sense to anyone else, in his crazed, overwhelmed state, it made sense to him.

In fact, he was so flustered that Owyhee Kenny had forgotten to put on pants.

Parts, gears, and belts spinning and humming beneath him. The vibrations of the engine pulsating throughout his body. The tractor was breathing on its own, exhaling its exhaust, piston spinning, spark plugs sparking.

Life was desperate for Owyhee Kenny. He had decided to carefully remove the governor, a part that he himself had installed. He got it by trading rye bread with the tractor man. The governor mechanism is what prevents vehicles from exceeding maximum speed even though the engine and gearing might allow it.

After about ten minutes, the part was removed. He climbed back atop the beast.

He gripped the steering wheel on both sides. His fingers, now white from how hard he was squeezing. Engaging the throttle ever so slowly, he built the speed up until it had reached maximum velocity.

Owyhee Kenny revved up the beast as fast as she could go. Ridey McTractor was traveling the same course that she always did. He sat atop this iron giant like a king on his throne. His knuckles ached from gripping the steering wheel. At normal speed hitting a 90-degree angle would be dangerous. With the governor removed, hitting a 90-degree angle was suicidal. The centrifugal force of the turn would cause the tractor to roll and Owyhee Kenny knew it.

58

And as he approached the 90-degree turn, there was a moment where he could have backed out.

He could opt-out at any moment.

There was that split second where he was struck with perfect clarity. A moment where the struggle between what is right and what is wrong is in perfect tension. He could end the charade immediately, all that he had to do was release the throttle.

Make no mistake, Owyhee Kenny was not suicidal, he wanted to live. However, he was scared of losing his potato farm, of having to start over, of losing the respect of his wife.

Owyhee Kenny was going to roll Ridey McTractor and hope for the best. So with both hands, Owyhee Kenny grabbed the steering wheel and yanked with all of his might.

As the tractor began its turn the centrifugal force pushed Kenny out of his seat. Because of the force of the turn, he was JUST hanging on to the steering wheel, nothing else was attached.

Then the unexpected happened. The front right tire hit a funny rut. It caused the steering wheel of the tractor to turn with such force and such speed that it was like the arm of a skeet shooter tossing Kenny up, up into the air and then down. Between the speed of the tractor and the torque of the steering wheel, Owyhee Kenny was flung roughly 100 paces from the tractor. This detail that Owyhee Kenny could neither have anticipated or planned for.

The tractor began to roll, three, four, five times. By the time the metal beast was finished, there was not much left of old Ridey McTractor. Parts were strewn in every direction. A machine that had served the family well all these years, was relegated to smoke, rubber and twisted metal.

 PRO TIP: A good used tractor runs about $20,000 in Idaho.

It was at this moment that Owyhee Kenny thought to himself, "This may not have been the most thought-out plan."

It was also too late.

There was additional pain for Owyhee Kenny by joining the gravity club. It was this unforeseen rut, that prompted the Superman audition. The rut also saved his life that day. If Owyhee Kenny had just been thrown off of the tractor, he would have been destroyed by the many rolls and flying debris that would have crushed him upon its landing. Instead, Owyhee Kenny was thrown completely free from the tractor's deluge,

Up until the moment that the tractor tire hit the rut, Owyhee Kenny was fixated on rolling it. He believed that the staged accident would fix everything.

When facing similar circumstances, many people become religious, others become philosophers, Owyhee Kenny was regretful. While his body toppled end over end, he knew that he had made a grave mistake. Now, he would have given anything to undo it all and come up with a better, less consequential plan.

Owyhee Kenny landed on a pile of potatoes. A detail that, for reasons of being "too obvious" will only be appreciated by book clubs and public readings of this book in hipster bookstores.

Owyhee Kenny was hurt, he had broken ribs, arms, legs but he was okay, or at least alive.

It hurt, a lot.
It hurt to move,
It hurt to breathe.
It hurt to lay still.
It hurt more than anything.
It just hurt.

Compounding the pain was the sense of seclusion. He was alone. In his heart, he knew that he had betrayed himself, his wife and his family. He was imprisoned in his own thoughts and pain. It was a feeling he would live through during his whole recovery.

His only comfort was Chompers who ran and found him and just laid down next to him. It was over. It was at this point that Owyhee Kenny closed his eyes and lost consciousness.

A Pile of Cotton and Shame

So many people live within unhappy circumstances and yet will not take the initiative to change their situation because they are conditioned to a life of security, conformity, and conservatism, all of which may appear to give one peace of mind, but in reality nothing is more dangerous to the adventurous spirit within a man than a secure future.

— Christopher McCandless

Owyhee Kenny and Chompers laid there in the potato pile for three hours. He fell in and out of consciousness. People started to look for him. Russ came upon a tractor laying in a heap strewn across the potato farm like a yard sale in a trailer park. Bits and pieces scattered here and there. The engine was still mostly running, or at least smoking. Russ screamed for his father, but there was no answer. For Russ, full-blown panic had set in.

After ten minutes of unbridled, hysteric searching, Russ could see an ankle and a tail. Owyhee Kenny laid. It was off in the distance, beside a pool of standing water and a pile of potatoes. Never had a son been so excited to see an ankle before. Russ tried to talk to his father but received silence in reply.

Owyhee Kenny was unconscious and unable to respond. Even if he were conscious, he couldn't respond because of his broken ribs.

His father was still breathing so he knew that he was alive, but he also knew that the situation was grim.

That day, Russ ran faster than he had ever run in his life. When he reached the farmhouse he was painfully out of breath. Once he got home, he called 9-1-1 on his family's rotary telephone. "ARG, that '9,' why couldn't my parents just buy a regular phone, or have a mobile phone like any respectable person in this day and age." As he waited for the nine to finish spinning, he had to find the one and then the one again.

His panic increased with each number dialed. He could feel his life and the life of his family fading until on the other end of the phone he could hear the 911 operator say "911 Operator how can I help you?" Suddenly, it felt like there was going to be some help.

Unfortunately, Russ was so out of breath,

that all he could muster was nonsensical gibberish, "Accident Farm Tractor." The 911 operator interrupted him and said, "Please slow down sir, it sounds like there was an accident. Where was this accident, sir?" Russ was just starting to slow down enough to be coherent when he said: "Farm Tractor Father Help."

One more time the 911 operator requested him to slow down, "I need you to slow down sir, we want to dispatch services to you, but need to know more about the situation."

Finally, Russ had his lungs restored enough to convey the following, "My Father, Owyhee Kenny was thrown from his tractor today on our family potato farm and he is very hurt, he is unconscious but breathing, we need an ambulance here immediately."

Russ went on to give the address of the farm.

The Ibaegurins had one mobile phone that they shared. You paid for use by the minute, so they weren't all chatty on it.

Russ called the families mobile phone. The phone was on vibrate and sitting inside Owyhee Kenny's coat pocket. The vibration was just enough to stir him to a half-conscious state. A place he entered for a split-second, long enough to feel the excruciating pain before returning to his darkness.

With no answer, Russ decided to just start calling everyone that might know where his mother was.

He called the church, she wasn't there.
He called the library, she wasn't there.
He called her friends, she wasn't with

them.

Finally, he called the grocery store and talked to a clerk. He said, "This is Russ Ibaiguren, my father was just in a tractor accident, I think that he may die, He is laying next to the shed, unconscious. I can't find my mom, her name is Dorothea, and she shops there. I have called everywhere else, can you help me find her?"

The clerk was clearly moved with compassion and said, "Yes, it is a bit unusual, but I can help you."

The clerk picked up the archaic handset to the store's intercom system. He pressed the button and began to talk. "Paging Dorothea Ibaiguren, your husband was just in a horrific tractor accident, he is unconscious, lying next to the shed. Your son is on the phone if you want to talk to him." Then there was a pause and he continued, "You should really get a mobile phone, they really aren't that expensive."

Then he continued, "Come to the customer service desk."

And that series of phone calls, culminated by the store announcement is how everyone in town learned that Owyhee Kenny was near death at the same time as Dorothea.

She was in the store that day and raced to the front where the clerk was just finishing his announcement.

Dorothea, desperately lunged for the phone and screamed into the mouthpiece, "Russ, what happened, where is your dad?"

Russ quickly re-explained the situation to his mom.

65

She said, "I will meet you at the hospital."

She dropped the phone so that it was hanging by its ringletted chord and ran to her car as fast as her hush puppy pumps would take her.

This is the exact same time that the ambulance arrived at the farm. Russ waived them down and directed them to where his father was lying unconscious.

Chompers was still there at Owyhee Kenny's side.

The EMTs assessed the situation as grim, and they worked meticulously to get Owyhee Kenny loaded onto the stretcher and then secured in the ambulance.

As soon as he was in the ambulance, they began to treat him for his ailments.

Russ jumped in the back of the ambulance with them. He was worried about his dad. There was a jump seat just inside the door where Russ sat down.

The EMT looked at him for a long second and said, "Please buckle up, it is the law."

Russ felt scolded.

Assessments were being performed on Owyhee Kenney. They put an oxygen mask on him and started an IV.

As the ambulance pulled away, Chompers still sat there in the field, no wag left to his tail.

Meanwhile, back in the grocery store parking lot, Dorothea had the unfortunate luck that her old blue truck would not start.

She needed to get to the hospital fast and the truck wouldn't start, as if to add fuel to the fire, there was traffic. If only she could get there with lights and sirens. Then she had an idea.

That was unfortunate for the 19-year old young man crammed into a large potato costume. He was at the local grocery store promoting Betta-Cola and having his picture taken with children.

Fate frowned on him that day as he had just entered Dorothea's angry field of vision

Standing at near seven feet tall, four feet around, and decked out in bright colors, the large potato's forced smile had become too much.

. Because of his limited field of view, he could not have known that a 40-year old woman was barreling at him, intoxicated by the need to protect her family.

She leaped at the large potatoes headfirst making herself prone to the ground laying what could be considered the kind of tackle reserved for professional football leagues.

The larger than life, cotton-filled potato was laid out, and unable to move without help. Dorothea took advantage of the situation where she climbed on top of it to tear out the stuffing and release the young man from his prison of fuzz.

She continued her staged hostilities toward the large tuber until an officer on patrol noticed the commotion.

The officer took her story and loaded her into the back of her police car. He showed compassion. Instead of taking her to the police station where she belonged, he took her to the hospital to see her husband.

Cold-Comfort

Chuck Norris doesn't go to church, Church comes to him.

- *Author unknown*

A few days had passed.

It was raining. The sound of raindrops hit the metal roof of Potato City Community Church. The sound echoed like a metal drum.

It was Baptism Sunday. The Baptismal was full of water. Pews were roped off so that the church felt more full.

In a small town, there are two places where you see everyone. You get caught up on life at the grocery store, and the community church. You don't have to go every Sunday to get the full scoop, but if you want to get the temperature show up.

The church building itself was large. It was built in a different era. In times past, everyone in the community went to this church. Whether it was the natural ebb and flow of congregants, or the upstart, hipper churches, the PCCC was never more than half full. Even with the drop-off in attendance, the church still understood its role in the community. It was a place for countless families that wanted to know and to be known by others.

The water was warm in the baptismal because Pastor Skip didn't like it cold. It was rumored that on more than one occasion, He had filled the baptismal with hot water and used it as the communal hot tub. The rumor is unsubstantiated, but there are members of the church who with the right coaxing would be able to describe the baptismal in much greater detail.

Hubba and Sparky both came to church this Sunday. They were both Christmas and Easter church attendees. The chance that they would both be in attendance on the same day that was not one of those Sundays meant something. They were both acutely aware of the current situation and their complicity in it.

Owyhee Kenny's accident hit Pastor Skip hard. He loved Owyhee Kenny and was greatly concerned about this special family.

Putting together and preaching a sermon this Sunday was one of the greatest challenges he had faced as clergy.

The following excerpt is a direct copy of Skip's notes that Sunday after the accident.

Friends, it is good to be with you all here today. We live in the greatest city, in the great state in the greatest country in the world. I truly believe that. [Pause, wait for response]. I am gonna do something different this morning. I had my sermon fully prepared, I was going to preach on the fruits of the Spirit again. I hope you remember them, they are out of Galatians 5

22 But the fruit of the Spirit is love, joy, peace, forbearance, kindness, goodness, faithfulness, **23** gentleness, and self-control.

The feeling here is that if you don't see these things in your life, then maybe, just maybe you are not the person that you think that you are. Where does that spring of life come from? The source? The hope? The purpose? The peace inside us, that is the reason you wake in the morning redeemed and rested, soundly.

We Christians are not perfect people, but we have a light, a compass, a direction. Such that, when we follow that light we know where we are going. As many of you know when you are hiking and the trail is not well marked, hikers will stack rocks as a marker for the trail. Those stacks of rocks are called Cairns. If you are lost, you look for the Cairns. They mark the trail. They mark the way in and the way back to safety.

Friends, the God of the universe stacked those rocks up, when he put skin on, came down to earth, lived, loved and died on this earth. His name was Jesus, at Christmas, we celebrate his birth and at Easter, we celebrate his resurrection. With his life, he said:

Do, as I do.
Be as I am.
Live as I live,
Hope as I hope.
Pray as I pray.

He was a living Cairn for us. A path that we could follow even when the trail was unclear. Friends, the path is often unclear, and that is why we look for the Cairns.

Last night one of our own had a tractor accident, Owyhee Kenny was driving his tractor and it flipped, the details are still sketchy, but we know that he is in the hospital and that his family is worried about him.

Our church gives a lot away already, and I know that many of you are facing some of the greatest financial challenges of your life, so I am not going to ask you to give more because you can't give what you don't have. But we serve a God who owns cattle on a thousand hillsides. Our God has more than enough and more than enough to share. I was praying over this last night and I had an idea, I believe that the Lord gave it to me and there are two parts to it.

Part 1: Cairns, I want you all to build cairns everywhere you go. Stack 'em up there. Stacks of rocks all over this great city, every time you see a stack of rocks, you are saying "I love Jesus and I support Owyhee Kenny," you are going to see these things multiply everywhere. EVERYWHERE. It is a quiet way of not letting your left hand know what your right hand is doing, in the early church they would draw the picture of the Jesus fish to identify as Christians I am asking you to stack rocks.

Part 2: A bottle drive. It is brilliant, at a nickel a bottle redemption value, you are not giving anything away that could benefit you. Then when other people see the Cairns and ask you how they can help, I want you to tell them to build Cairns and collect bottles.

71

This community cares for each other, and this is a simple way we can help Kenny's family. Bring the bottles by the church here and just put them in the Storage building. When we fill that up, we will find a bigger place to store them.

This gesture is the embodiment of this scripture about the fruits of the spirit. We are living out "Love" in big, bold letters.

After the service, Sparky made a beeline for Hubba a.k.a. Mr. Potato Head. Everyone in the church was drinking coffee and eating sandwich cookies. They made small talk about pee-wee football, lawn care, and motorcycles. Meanwhile, Sparky and Hubba were quite concerned. They found each other.

Sparky said, "Was that us?"

Hubba was as confused as Sparky and said, "I don't know, it IS the kind of thing that we do, do. There is a large metal dinosaur that we left on their front porch."

Sparky quickly responded, "Yes, I know about the T-rex, we can make up a story, local PD will comply. Did we sabotage that tractor? Attempted murder is a whole different level." Hubba didn't know and was not going to pretend that he did, so he said, "Safe answer, Yes, the real answer, I have no idea, could have been one of the potatoes just letting off some steam." Sparky, concerned about liability and unraveling all of his evil plans that he had worked so long and hard on said "Letting off steam, by almost killing the farm owner, that seems excessive.

72

This is unacceptable, we almost had him and now we have to change the plan."

Hubba, trying to put things back together said, "Look, I know this is tough right now, I will talk to the guys."

Sparky, who was quite concerned and visually disturbed, asserted, "You will do no such thing, this has to go away."

At this point, the two men were interrupted by a blue-haired lady, who was in the throes of dementia. She interrupted both men saying, "You know, I can hear everything that you are saying."

This statement was dementia speaking. It was not a coherent understanding of anything. Sparky and Mr. Potato Head interpreted this statement as though they were found out. They believed that she HAD heard everything and understood it. She then wandered onto the next person. If Sparky and Hubba had kept listening, they would have heard her claim that she rode a reindeer in the Macy's Thanksgiving Day Parade dressed as a canned ham, which also was not true.

Sparky and Hubba were spooked.

Sparky immediately said, "We can't talk here," to which

Hubba replied, "We can't talk anywhere if this gets found out, and we are going to go to jail."

Sparky, the resident psychopath offered up comfort, "We aren't going to go to jail, but we have to make this go away."

Still, in fixing mode, Hubba asked the question "Should we get rid of old Blue Hair?"

The issue was Owyhee Kenny and not some blue-haired lady, and Sparky knew it, so he commanded "No, No, I will fix this with Owyhee Kenny. You have done enough already. This is a liability, your team is a liability."

Hubba responded, "Got it, so, to clarify, no talking, no killing Owyhee Kenny."

A bit surprised by the question, Sparky offered a trite response "Correct on both counts. No killing of anyone."

As each congregant went home, they were greeted leaving the parking lot with a Cairn. One that Pastor Skip had erected that morning between raindrops to remind each person that they were part of something bigger. Each person went home and marked their homes with a Cairn. They went on to build more and more cairns all over the community.

Workplaces, grocery stores, veterinary clinics, there were cairns everywhere. Other people started to ask about them.

The bottle drive also started to take form. Bottles started to arrive at the church, and the storage building filled up faster than anyone could have imagined. An empty industrial warehouse was donated to house all of the extra bottles.

The generosity of the community poured out, but it was cold-comfort for the family sitting bedside with the patriarch praying that he was going to survive.

One Stupid Bloke

Health is the greatest gift, contentment the greatest wealth, faithfulness the best relationship.

-Buddha

Days passed, It was dark and Owyhee Kenny was strapped down in a hospital bed. His arms and legs wrapped tight. He was medicated and couldn't feel anything but pressure.

After what felt like a lifetime, Owyhee Kenny decided to open his eyes. He had taken stock of every decision that had led up to this point. He knew that he had to face the consequences of his actions.

As life came into focus, a nurse named Megan whispered, "He is awake." She was a dedicated nurse that Big Potato had assigned to his bedside. Although she was on the payroll of Big Potato, she was a healer, not a political pawn.

PRO TIP: The most popular name for a nurse in the United States is Megan. If your name is Megan, you should consider going into the nursing profession.

The SIPC hired Nurse Megan because there were big concerns from the community, law enforcement and within the organization that they had sabotaged Owyhee Kenny's tractor. Frankly, no one could deny the allegation. Sparky couldn't. The SIPC and the potato heads had done this kind of thing before. Big Potato had been set up perfectly, and rather than deny the claims, the SIPC decided to acknowledge their involvement through the hiring of Nurse Megan.

To provide comfort, Nurse Megan stroked Owyhee Kenny's hair. In his half-groggy state, she comforted him that everything was going to be okay.

She told him, "You are lucky to be alive. Your son found you in a potato field, unconscious. You were thrown from your tractor on a 90-degree turn. It appeared that some critical throttle systems had failed. Please don't worry about the 'How this happened' right now. You have to focus on your healing." She continued, "You have been unconscious or hopped up on drugs for three days. The Southeast Idaho Potato Council is looking for the parts because they wanted to go after the tractor manufacturer for this gross neglect. I know that Sparky would like to come to visit you personally. Because he personally knows you and believes that you are such an important part of this community, the Southeast Idaho Potato Council would like to pay for all of your medical bills. He asked me to contact him as soon as you were awake. Do you feel like you are ready for company?"

As Owyhee Kenny concentrated on his breathing, inhaling and exhaling, he started to realize what was taking place. With each breath, he was exhaling out the hurt, frustration, and resentment that had grown over the years. And he inhaled life-renewing energy.

Although his body was broken, his spirit was alive. He felt stronger than he had ever been. So, at long last, Owyhee Kenny acquiesced and offered to see Sparky, but would like to see his wife and son first.

Nurse Megan immediately went into the hallway to find Russ and Dorothea.

Russ came in first, tears ran down his raw cheeks. It was Russ who ran home at full speed and called 911, who waited for the ambulance and who rode to the hospital with his father that night.

That night was Russ's eagle feather. He grew up to be a man, a task that you can only do when you are faced with that level of trauma. Russ came of age. As he contemplated what life would be like without his father, a stalwart man that could handle anything, Russ cried. And each hour that passed brought a greater reality of what life might look like without his father. His cheeks were raw from tears. He was tired of crying. This moment, as he walked into the hospital room, he saw his father looking healthier than he had ever been. Because although he was strapped down with every medical device imaginable, you could see in his eyes that he was liberated. Probably the first time that Russ had seen his father free. Russ hugged his father, his father could not hug back but sat there with his son, and the two men cried.

And then Russ spoke, "Dad, I thought that you were dead. When I came upon you in the field, the tractor had tipped over on its side, there was smoke, and I couldn't find you. I was so scared. At that point that I had to remember to breathe. I promised God that I would be good from now on if I could just find you. It is so weird, it sounds like the whole accident was a setup. I am just so glad that you are okay. I do have one question though for you." Owyhee Kenny responded, "What is it son?" and without missing a beat Russ responded, "When I found you, you weren't wearing any pants, why were you not wearing pants?"

The real answer is that Owyhee Kenny just forgot to put them on that day. The elite, intelligent types sometimes are so caught up in their own heads that they forget to do some of the most obvious things like wearing pants. He had been so stuck in his head that he had completely forgotten to put the pants on. The answer that he provided Russ was that he was still recovering from his accident and he doesn't remember anything about pants.

Dorothea had gone to the cafeteria to get

some lukewarm carved turkey and some mashed potatoes with gravy. She was unaware that her husband was wide-awake.

To her astonishment, Owyhee Kenny was awake and asking about her. She came upstairs and sit by him holding hands. Any attempt that she made to talk ended up in tears careening down her face.

Owyhee Kenny had things to say, though. He didn't want to share anything with her that could incriminate her. However, he needed to share, so he did his best, "Dorothea, I have something to share with you, something that I am not proud of and something that I can't completely share. I have never ever not been truthful with you, which is why this is so hard for me."

Dorothea nodded along acknowledging that she understood, and Owyhee Kenny continued, "I have to confess to you that I have not been completely honest with you. You know about the SIPC and the squeeze that they are putting on us. Well, this year is worse, it is way worse. We have no money and Sparky is squeezing harder than he ever has before. I should have told you. I was wrong by not including you in all of the information. Can you forgive me?"

Dorothea loved Owyhee Kenney with the deepest love that a woman can have for a man. She worked up her composure and said "Owyhee Kenny, you stupid, stupid bloke, of course, I forgive you, but I am pretty hot at you this moment. I will always forgive you. I will always think the best of you, but I can't help you if you don't talk to me."

She continued, "I have never been more scared in my life. I thought you were dead, whatever you did was not worth the chance of possibly losing you. There are always other plans and other ideas. I love you, I have your back, and I forgive you."

After about 15 minutes, she added, "I may have accosted a large potato at the grocery store today. The police came and pulled me off. All that was left was a pile of stuffing."

"Why," Owyhee Kenny responded.

"The car wouldn't start."

Having been married to Dorothea for long enough he knew not to probe, so he just responded, "We need to get the truck looked at."

"Yep"

She continued to sit in the hospital room, mostly silent, for the next three hours. That was until Pastor Skip showed up.

Pastor Skip prayed for Owyhee Kenny and offered his support. He mentioned that there were many people at Church on Sunday that were concerned and want to help. He mentioned the Cairns that they were all over town. In fact, from Owyhee Kenny's hospital room, in every direction, there were piles of rocks. He continued, "The community couldn't do much, so they built cairns as a remembrance for you. They really love you. We are all so glad that you are okay."

The door creaked as it opened, Sparky had arrived. Sparky believed that the tractor accident was 100% the fault of Big Potato. His job was to fix things. He greeted Pastor Skip and politely

81

waited for Pastor Skip to note the discomfort and excuse himself. The response from Pastor Skip did not take long.

 PRO TIP: Being evil isn't easy. Find a mentor, do your homework, be prepared.

Pastor Skip put his hand on Owyhee Kenny's shoulder and said, "Look, I have to go, we will keep the prayers coming, Please get better quickly" And with that Pastor Skip and Dorothea left the room.

There was nothing altruistic about this visit. He wanted two things. First, he wanted damage control. He wanted to know and control anything that could link the tractor accident back to the SIPC and he wanted leverage.

Although the two men had known each other for a very long time, Sparky was a pro, he understood the current emotional aptitude of his adversary.

Owyhee Kenny knew Sparky too, so the visit is no surprise.

Sparky looked Owyhee Kenny in the eye, "Kenneth, I just first want to say that we are just so happy that you are alive. I know that you have a lot to think about right now. I know that we were playing hardball with you, and I just wanted you to know that we can talk about all of that later. Right now, we just want you to focus on your healing. We want to make sure that you and your family are taken care of. That is why we are taking care of ALL of your hospital bills

AND we are going to hire a grief counselor and tutor for Russ to help him process all of the difficult emotions we believe he is experiencing. We have contacted the school and let them know what is going on and they are making every accommodation to make sure Russ will not be penalized in school because of this horrible tragedy. We also have a team of investigators looking into this egregious situation trying to identify exactly what happened to you and what steps can be taken in the future to prevent this type of tragedy from happening to someone else."

Owyhee Kenny, with keen perception, replied, "Well, that is mighty kind of you Sparky, none of that is necessary, it is appreciated but not necessary." Sparky responded, "Listen, if there is anything that you need, ANYTHING, please just let us know, Nurse Megan knows how to get a hold of us anytime. You have all of the resources of the Southeast Idaho Potato Council at your disposal. Again, just don't worry about any of the farm discussion, we can revisit that once you are healthy. For now, just focus on getting better and loving your family "

There was a flicker in Owyhee Kenny's eye, "You know there is one thing that you could do." A bit surprised, Sparky replied, "Name it."

Owyhee Kenny was surprised by the sudden change in Sparky and Big Potato. Because it was so new and different, he didn't trust it and wanted to test it out a bit. Owyhee Kenny was not vindictive, he just wanted what was fair. He also wanted to understand why Big Potato was being SOOOOOO nice. So this is why the remainder of the conversation turns weird.

"I want an in-ground pool," Owyhee Kenny told Sparky. He continued "Yes sir, an in-ground pool, I would like a pool that you can swim in. I would like an in-ground pool that the community can come to and swim. I want to be able to invite the church over for swimming Thursdays and I want toddlers in the preschool class to learn to swim here and I want blue-haired ladies to exercise in the shallow end of the pool. I want a pool"

Sparky wasn't sure how to respond, it was a strange request, but a small cost versus the responsibility of owning the cost of the accident. Sparky responded, "Then a pool you will have. Is that it?"

Owyhee Kenny thought he would push it just a little bit farther, "Yes sir, and a diving board." To which Sparky replied, "Then your pool will have a diving board."

Sparky would make good on his promises that day, albeit none for the right reason. And as a case-study for the importance of irony, Sparky hired a team of potato workers to work Kenny's potato farm while Owyhee Kenny was re-cooperating in the hospital. The tractor was fixed, and an in-ground pool was carved into the landscape of the property just below the house.

Although Owyhee Kenny's hospital bills would be covered and the damage to the farm would be repaired, Owyhee Kenny was still underwater financially. He knew that he would still have to sell his farm and Big Potato would win. The cards were stacked against him. He had no other options but he had purchased his family some time with his "accident".

He could see what could only be stacks of rocks rising out of deep pools of rainwater in all directions. It was comforting. As he drifted off to sleep that night in his hospital bed, for the first time in a long time, he had hope.

Federal Potato Investigators

In West Virginia yesterday, a man was arrested for stealing several blow-up dolls. Reportedly, police didn't have any trouble catching the man because he was completely out of breath.
-        *Conan O'Brien*

In this community, the word "police" may be a bit of misnomer. By appearance, the Blackfoot Police Department could have been restaurateurs or auto-mechanics. Their appearance displayed the tousled hair and unkempt look.

Their appearance was not the issue. They are corrupt. They have been purchased.

The bottom line was that the SIPC runs the town and Sparky runs the SIPC. Sparky picked who would be elected, who would be appointed, and who would be squeezed. Sparky hand-picked the police chief and the whole staff.

Sparky was the definition of corrupt by which corruption should be measured. At some level in his psychopathy, he enjoyed the misery that he inflicted. If there was something that Sparky needed the police for, they were there. If there was something that he wanted to keep the police out of, they were conveniently too busy doing other things.

Owyhee Kenny's accident is the type of event that normal police would investigate. They would come to the hospital room to check on Owyhee Kenny. They would take a statement from him.

They did not.

Those visitors did not come to visit Owyhee Kenny, and because it was Blackfoot, no one expected them to.

When a gentleman in a dark suit donned the door of Owyhee Kenny's hospital room, it was a bit of surprise.

A low, sullen voice broke the silence, "Kenneth Ibaiguren, my name is Kyle Pierce.... And I work with the Federal... "

Owyhee Kenny, still a bit groggy but with enough cognition to interrupt said, "Bureau of Investigation, someone called the FBI over our little tractor mishap! Great day in the morning if I ever thought that I would see the day. Also, call me Owyhee Kenny. The name 'Kenneth' is reserved for my tombstone."

Kyle Pierce waited for Owyhee Kenny to stop talking to say, "Investigation, no just a little different from that, I work with the Federal Potato Investigators, it is *also* a federal agency, but are housed under the United States Department of Agriculture. The name was such a bad name choice. It fuels so many jokes in DC. Someone, somewhere thought that the confusion between the names would be funny. So now, because of that person, here I am representing the FPI."

Owyhee Kenny replied "Well, I'll be, it is still pretty exciting to get someone out from the FPI to talk to us. What can I do for you today sir?"

Kyle Pierce started to pour himself a glass of water. He continued, "Listen, I'm out of Salt Lake City. We have jurisdiction over Blackfoot. The Southeast Idaho Potato Council has shown up on our radar and we are trying to better understand the organization."

Owyhee Kenny asked, "Are you here to talk about the Tractor Accident?"

"Well, yes sir, I am." Kyle Pierce replied.

Owyhee Kenny said, "There isn't much to say. I was working the field, and the next thing that I knew, I was here in the hospital. I wish that I could help you more."

Owyhee Kenney knew that he had set up the tractor accident AND had just given the Southeast Idaho Potato Council just about enough grief on the matter.

No one likes a snitch and Kenny knew this. He knew that he couldn't roll over on the SIPC, for valid reasons:

First, he had sabotaged himself on the tractor. In this case, the SIPC was blameless.

Additional attention brought to the tractor accident was attention that he didn't need. There is nothing illegal about getting into a tractor accident on purpose. It did introduce questions that he did not want to answer.

Second, even if Big Potato had been involved in the big tractor accident, rolling over and snitching on the council would be an automatic recipe for bankruptcy, or worse.

Good potato farming folks in the past had talked to attorneys and law enforcement. It ALWAYS got back to the council. If you are going to take a shot at the council, make it a kill-shot.

Lastly, the visitor log at the hospital would show this visitor, and so there would be some positive collateral he might want to use later. Not to mention that there was a dedicated nurse to manage his care that was being provided by the SIPC. She was dedicated to Owyhee Kenny's health, but she was listening. Anything that he said to the FPI was like saying it directly to the SIPC.

So Owyhee Kenny had some choices about how we would respond. In this case, the choice was easy.

Kyle Pierce stood there waiting for a response. Finally, Owyhee Kenny broke the silence and said "I am sorry that you came all the way from Salt Lake to see me, but really all that I remember was that I was working on the tractor and then the very next thing that I remember was waking up here. I wish that I had more to share with you, but I don't so I must say good day to you." Kyle objected pulling a 2 by 3.5-inch business card out of his wallet saying,

"Listen, I know that you have a lot going on, I am going to leave my business card right here on this shelf, if you think of anything at all, please call me."

Owyhee Kenny smiled his signature half-crooked smile and thanked Kyle for coming. This was probably why Kyle Pierce stood there like a deer in headlights wringing his hands and said, "I do appreciate anything that you can remember." And he walked out effectively ending the investigation before it even started and any hope of outside help.

Trench Mouth

*I told my dentist my teeth are going
yellow, he told me to wear a brown tie.*
- Rodney Dangerfield

Everyone has teeth, or at least, everyone
starts with teeth.

Sparky did.

His teeth hurt...

A lot.

He went to the dentist because his mouth
was aching.

He arrived early. Pictures drawn by
children's hands were framed and hung around
the lobby. Rows of couches framed in by old
copies of Sports Illustrated and People
magazines. The waiting room was full. People sat
there in a trance-like conditions waiting to be
called back to the chair.

Sparky checked in at the front desk and then waited. As he waited, he looked around the room and saw children with runny noses and old people with coughs. He didn't like germs, he was not happy.

At long last, it was his turn to meet with his dentist. Dr. Sam Burns, nearing retirement, was reducing his number of patients. He was ready for the easy life of playing with his grandkids and his model train collection.

Sparky, bothered, was ushered back to the dental chair, past the neutral tones of the walls that were accented by the bright colors of the children's pictures. The lights were long, tired neon tubes illuminating the edges and corners of the room. The drill, ultrasonic hydra-pick, and laughing-gas mask were sitting at the ready. He climbed into the chair and waited.

As time passed, he felt like every other patient was seen before him. The dentist would pop into the adjacent room and talk about all matters unrelated to dentistry. Then the same thing, two rooms away.

At long last, the dentist arrive in Sparky's tooth station. A balloon blocked the dentist's view. Pushing it aside, he squared up to Sparky, eye to eye and said, "Hey Sparky, sounds like your teeth are hurting, how can we help today?"

Sparky shared, "I feel like a swallowed a swarm of angry bees. They are all stinging the inside of my mouth. I am ready to pull my teeth out myself. It is like there is a constant pain, no matter what I do."

Dr. Burns, offering a calm, but chipper, bedside manner said, "Let's see what is going on" and began to tip Sparky's chair back. He turned the spotlight on. The light both lit up Sparky's mouth and also revealed all of the wrinkles and scars that Sparky had accumulated over the years on his face.

"Mmm hmmm, Mmm hmmm, Mmm hmmm, yeah, Mmm hmmm, yep."

Without looking for a response, Dr. Burns continued to bring nonsensical conversations where he would ask questions and then personally answer them. "You like the Betta-Cola? I get so many people in here with bad teeth because of the Betta, because of the sugar beets they think it is healthy for them. I love the stuff personally, but every time I hear a can cracking open, I hear the sound of money."

His mirror shot around Sparky's mouth with an authority that only comes with a lifetime of service. He continued, "Okay, Okay, Yep, Yep, Okay".

He then turned off the spotlight shining in Sparky's mouth, tipped his chair upright and said, "Good news, there is nothing that I can do for you today. You have trench mouth. It is all psychological, well not really psychological, it is a stress response for your gums. You will need to reduce stress, take some Tylenol. Any good books on your list? I love to read. Maybe start running. Any friends with a hot tub? Do you like wine? I love wine, I don't understand it though, I just buy what the sommelier tells me to buy."

Sparky, now containing his anger, calmly stated, "You can't do anything?"

Dr. Burns tipped his head a bit askew and said, "Nothing, sorry. You can rinse your mouth

94

with salt-water, that may help a bit. Floss. I can make an introduction to my sommelier"

Sparky, stood up, holding his mouth with his right hand and said, "Well this was a waste of time."

As he left, he walked past the receptionist and through the lobby. He got to the parking lot and it was empty.

Sparky lost control. The monster inside took over.

With no effect, he grabbed a wrench out of his automotive tool kit and rushed to the propane tank, next to the building. Propane valves are reverse threaded and are low-pressure, so a standard wrench will work. He loosened the connection until he could smell propane and then loosened it more.

Throwing his wrench in his pocket. He grabbed a book of matches and as he walked away, he muttered, "Sayonara Spud!" He struck one match and threw it over his right shoulder. The match caught the stream of propane and immediately set it ablaze.

Sparky rushed to his car and drove away. No one saw anything.

The fire spread quickly through the dental office causing fire alarms to go off and staff and patients alike to panic. Everyone rushed to the exits but were OK.

By the time the fire department arrived at the dentist office, the building was gone. No one was injured, but the building was gone.

Meanwhile, Sparky was safely back at the SIPC, sitting at his desk playing minesweeper.

A New Normal

"The shepherd drives the wolf from the sheep's throat, for which the sheep thanks the shepherd as his liberator, while the wolf denounces him for the same act as the destroyer of liberty."
— Abraham Lincoln

Months had passed, life had quickly changed for young Russ. He found his father near death after the tractor accident. That event had emotional consequences.

He lived through his father's recovery. He had the growing awareness that their family would lose the Farm.

These events accelerated his adolescent development. Naiveté is a luxury of the affluent. The Ibaiguerns were not wealthy, they were trading pumpernickel for shoes. Thriftiness in his family was a virtue that was held in the

96

highest regard.

The bills folder that kept getting larger. The family was in financial crisis.

It was the culmination of circumstances that created the astringent conditions. Ultimately, it was the accident that forced Russ's enlightenment.

This awareness brought new feelings and thoughts. He was a person in conflict and needed a guide.

Russ was spending more and more time with his guidance counselor, Ms. Yamada. She was quite old and each year that passed considered retirement just a little bit more. A woman who always looked for extra ways to take care of this kid. She took Russ and his friends bowling, and out to dinner. But best of all, she listened to Russ's fears and hopes.

Big Potato did call the school to tie up any and all loose ends. Ms. Yamada always answered the phone when Big Potato called. With everything going on, she heard a desperate, guilty organization trying to protect itself. They wanted to buy off a family that had just undergone a tragedy. Big Potato made her sick and she wanted absolutely nothing to do with them. However, there was this impressive, innocent kid, Russ. Big Potato asked her to look after Russ. Something that she was already doing, but also, something that if it ever got out would make Ms. Yamada appear to be, at best, disingenuous, and at worst complicit.

Ms. Yamada hired the tutors for Russ. She planned special field trips to the places that he knew that Russ and his friends would like visiting.

They went to the clock tower at Ann Morrison Park in Boise. She took a group rafting down the Snake River in Hells Canyon. The goal was to get Russ out of his funk and to have Big Potato pay for it.

Russ thought that he was going to lose his father. The loss that Russ was most afraid of, is the very thing that saved his father. The moment that Owyhee Kenny was thrown from that tractor was a chrysalis. He was like a butterfly emerging from its cocoon.

The irony of Owyhee Kenny's real life makes for great storytelling, but does not comfort a young man who is struggling because he almost lost his father.

Time.

Time is what Russ needed to heal.

He needed time to ride bikes and skip rocks and throw them at a target for hours on end while sipping ice tea. He needed to be a kid, but Russ couldn't be a kid anymore, that had been stolen from him. So Russ didn't know what to do.

Ms. Yamada saw this tension in Russ and invited him to the counseling office where she shared her story with him. Ms. Yamada said, "Russ, you know that I am a Japanese American? Did you know that my family was brought to Idaho as part of the Japanese Internment camps? My family was from Bainbridge Island, Washington. In 1941, we moved to Idaho because of the color of my skin and my family's national heritage."

There was irony in this, that year, 1941,

thousands of Japanese families were forced to move east of the Idaho/Washington border, and if the families were to refuse to move, they were rounded it up and moved to internment camps in Idaho. Ms. Yamada's family had opted to move voluntarily to Idaho.

Ms. Yamada went on, "Our lives were not in danger but we felt ashamed about our heritage. We felt unclean. It was dirt so deep that we couldn't wash it off. We had to live with it. I don't mean to trivialize your experience or my family's experience and say that it is the same thing. That would be unfair but, I do know what it feels like to grow up suddenly. Our family went from finding crabs on the beach, to a life in a new community because of the color of my skin. My childhood was taken from me. Do you feel like your childhood was taken from you?"

"Yeah, I think I do, all of it. All of the things that you said, is what I am feeling. All of the things that I used to do, now just feel empty. I know our farm is in trouble; I see the bills stacking up. We used to go out to dinner, now all we eat is potatoes and whatever else my mom can grow," Russ replied.

Ms. Yamada eased into her reply, "My experience meant that there was a new normal for me. My childhood had transitioned into this new thing that I didn't understand, it was new and it was different AND it took some getting used to. We don't have to understand everything all the time. Sometimes we can just rest in the fact that we are who God created us to be and that is enough."

With the voice barely even audible, Russ asked, "How long did it take?" Ms. Yamada leaned in and responded matching his volume, "How long did what take?"

Now more confident, Russ asked, "You know, where you have a new normal, and start to feel like normal, normal?"

There was a pause; She was thinking. This conversation was magical and she knew it.

Finally, Ms. Yamada said, "Honestly, it still doesn't feel normal, normal. Something was taken from me in those years, and I realize that that may sound a bit depressing, but it isn't. It doesn't feel normal. It shouldn't feel normal. Maybe it was the first sin with the snake and the apple in the Garden of Eden. What I experienced was racism, and it was engineered by my country of birth. That shouldn't feel good. It should not ever feel good. And, it should never ever feel normal. What you experience with your dad and what feels very much like corporate coercion should not ever feel good, it should never feel normal. But it will begin to feel familiar, and that is almost enough."

Russ was confused, "When will familiar come?" he asked.

Ms. Yamada was aware of the gravity of the conversation, so she carefully constructed the following, "Familiar is like moving to a new city, where you don't know anyone or anything and you hurt over leaving the place that you come from. Each day you grimace as you walk past the same old shops and people and just when you're ready to run away from that place as fast as you can, that place starts to feel familiar. Then those same shops and people become your shops and people. This new normal that we are talking about; you will run away from this, push away, you will do everything that you can do to escape this feeling, and then after you have given up the fight, it will be familiar. There are ways to make it a little easier."

Russ was tracking everything and wanted a lifeline, something that could help him apply some order to his chaos. "But, how can I make this easier," he asked.

The lifeline didn't come.

"Well, kid gloves for starters, you have to be patient with yourself, you can't be too hard on yourself, you are undergoing a major transition. Your entire worldview has shifted, and there are still a lot of things to understand. And find something that you care about. Make the world a better place. I know that it may sound 'Pollyanna,' but if you can find that thing that brings you hope and purpose, you can rise from the healing pools of Bethesda a new and changed person."

In the Bible, there was a crippled man who sat by the pools at Bethesda. There was a belief that any time that the water was stirred if you could get into the water, you would be healed. The problem was that he couldn't get into the pool by himself. The problem for Russ was that he couldn't figure this situation out on his own. So he asked, "How do I find that thing?"

Ms. Yamada smiled with her entire body. Her eyes, ears, nose, mouth, arms, and posture. At this point, the power in all of Idaho could have gone out, and the light that was emitted from Ms. Yamada's face could have lit up the entire state. And that was when she said, "That is the easy part, you try."

Advice that could be considered the easiest, most obvious advice anyone had ever received, or the most difficult, challenging call to action that had ever been issued.

Russ got it, he said "Okay" and then said it again and again and again. And then Ms. Yamada closed the conversation by saying "Okay" as well.

When you enter into the filth of someone's life, you are changed as well, and Ms. Yamada understood the honor of being asked the questions.

Russ wanted to be different, he wanted life to get easier, he wanted to try. So with a new outlook on life, Russ left Ms. Yamada's office that day looking for how he could put his new found perspective into action.

Blue Haired Purpose

*"Rocks in my path? I keep them all. With
them, I shall build my castle."*

— Nemo Nox

School was out, and after Russ's conversation
with Ms. Yamada, he headed home. While Russ
waited for the city bus home, a little old lady
with blue hair wheeled past on her ez-go scooter.
She had just been shopping and her basket was
full of potato chips packaged in a round cans.
There was also an ungodly amount and variety
of sandwich meat. She was old, and she was set
in her ways. She liked, what she liked. And just
as the scooter was cresting the hill out of site,
Russ developed an idea, he stood up and ran to
her.

Ez-go scooters travel slowly. They are
made to help the elderly be more mobile. When
not on an uphill slope, you might get saunter-

speed walk out of it. It was still off in the distance. When he caught up to her he was out of breath. He was wearing shoes, but out of breath.

He word-vomited, "You me running help me you purpose." It happened again, Russ had confused words because he had been running.

This was the same blue-haired lady from the church and the same lady who years earlier worked at the bank, and helped save Hubba's mom's life.

Old blue-hair was suffering from dementia. Russ's previous bout with incoherence passed right by. Russ missed a lot of social cues, but he was smart enough to understand what was going on with this lady. His trip up the hill to talk to this woman was not about being understood, but to understand. This was about being present. The same thing that Ms. Yamada had done for him.

Russ continued to walk alongside the ez-go scooter as the woman wouldn't slow down. It was an awkward gesture chasing the woman until she finally stopped. Coherence was not her strong suit: reality one minute talking about her son, the tugboat captain, and the next recalling the names of each tree in the park. The story didn't matter, everyone deserves to be heard and Russ listened.

The blue-haired lady offered Russ Betta-Cola and a Pringle sandwich. More importantly, she offered him blue-haired purpose. The two sat, roadside for the better part of an hour eating Pringle sandwiches and listening to the stories.

The good or bad news depending on your perspective is that she had a variety of potato chips and an inordinate amount of lunch meat options. For example try mixing and matching some olive loaf, with Pumpkin Spice potato chips. At first blush, this might sound bad, but the word "Bad" does not begin to explain what took place in Russ's mouth. It was a 50-car pileup, and emergency vehicles couldn't arrive to fix anything. Russ ate the potato chip, lunch meat sandwich, ate the whole thing and then asked for another.

 PRO TIP: Wasabi and Soy Sauce Pringles with a Pastrami Kicker.

As the two people sat there indulging on potato chips, lunch-meat sandwiches, a car rolled past and inside the car, Sparky offering his stair of death. The villain took special note that the older woman with blue hair had previously shared with Sparky at Church that she knew what he was doing and although this was the rant of a somewhat delusional old woman, Sparky now believed it to be true.

Then as he rolled past the only two people in the world that could potentially thwart his plan. He realized that he needed to do something, quick. In spite of being the center of two weird situations, the woman with blue hair, because of her dementia posed no risk to him.

Sparky usually had other people do his bidding. It was cleaner that way. He was smart. He didn't want anything to stick to him. He was teflon. He was careful, that there were clear separations of responsibility. This separation kept him safe. It kept everyone safe.

For Sparky, doing something means calling someone, and having them do something. Sparky called Hubba, Mr. Potato Head himself, and said, "Listen, I need you to do something for me. The old lady with blue hair and the kid we're talking. I was driving and saw the two of them laughing, so I pulled the car over. They must have talked for 30 minutes. Listen, we have to do something!"

Sparky paused, then continued, "I don't want you to hurt the kid and let me be very clear, this is not a job for the potato heads, I want you to handle this personally. The kid needs to disappear for a bit. Can you make him disappear? He is not to be harmed, that is too messy. I just want him out of play for a bit. I want the community to sweat for a bit. This young man cannot destroy everything that we have been working for. We have to contain him. Don't rough him up, honestly, don't even make him aware that you are taking him, just make him disappear for a bit."

Just as Sparky was finishing his phone call, it started to rain. Russ was grateful for the rain, his mouth and his digestive health were grateful for the rain.

Russ walked back to the bus stop unaware of the magnitude of what had just taken place in his heart, and unaware of what had taken place in the car across the street. As he walked home, he was recalling how he ended up listening to the blue-haired women ramble on about how she's been able to perfect the Turkey that goes into Turkish delight. As he was thinking about his new lease on life, Mr. Potato Head, a.k.a. Hubba was figuring out how to help the Kid disappear.

Meanwhile, as soon as Russ was out of sight. On this country road, Sparky got out of the car, unplugged the power source on the scooter and drove away immediately. She sat there roadside until the care facility sent out a search party.

That night, Russ opened his books and did his homework, unaware of what befell the blue-haired woman.

Things were different for him. Now the homework was still a bit stale, and his life a bit like a steamroller had rolled over the top of him, backed it up and rolled over the top of him again.

Hubba, on the other hand, was weighed down heavy about this kidnapping thing. Up until this moment, they had taken liberties with the law. They had not lowered themselves to kidnapping. The SIPC had fantastic legal representation and the courts were already owned and appointed by the council. In all of the legal battles, there had been zero convictions and the belief was that there never would be. Kidnapping was new. This was federal. And those courts were not owned by the SIPC.

There was one thing that kept Hubba at the SIPC. Sparky, so many years ago, was able to get Hubba's mother cancer treatment and retain management of the potato farm for his family through the SIPC.

Loyalty will get you far. On the long list of things that Hubba would do, none of them included kidnapping.

Hubba no longer liked his job. He didn't like to intimidate people. He to teach it to the underlings. He was in a rut.

He was in the 'tween' time.

The time between who he was and who he was becoming and this event was a catalyst for a change.

Hubba didn't sleep that night. He tried. He laid down. He closed his eyes. All that happened was that he studied the back of his eyelids and thought about federal prison.

Morning came all too early for Hubba. It was Saturday, and Hubba had to make a decision. He walked out to his, now aging, off-brand sports car. He turned it on and started to drive over to Russ's house.

The plan, however ill-conceived, was to get there and just talk to the boy. As the car got closer and closer, Hubba became more and more aware that his ill-conceived plan was empty.

The fact that the wheels stayed in a straight line is nothing short of a miracle. This sleep-deprived, stressed-out, anxiety-controlled man was on his way to do the most horrifying thing in his life.

Hubba rolled up on the Potato farm and saw Russ outside. Game time, he executed his ill-conceived plan. He would talk to him about the whole kidnapping thing. Hubba rolled his window down and said, "Hey Russ, I don't know if you remember me or not, we have met a couple of times."

Russ responded, "Sure, I remember you, you work with the Southeast Idaho Potato Council."

Hubba went on, "Listen, I know that this is probably going to come out pretty weird, so rather than just beat around the bush, I thought I would just come out and ask... or at least talk to you about it. See, here's the thing. The SIPC is trying to take your farm from you, and when your dad was thrown from the tractor, well, we think that that was us, so we are trying to clean up this whole mess, and then yesterday we saw you talking to a lady with blue hair, who somehow had a magical understanding of all things that take place in Southeast Idaho. Anyway, I was asked to make you disappear, so that is why I am here."

Puzzled, Russ asked, "Are you asking to kidnap me? I don't think it works that way." To which Hubba responded, "Um, yeah, I mean, that would be great, can I kidnap you?"

Voluntary Kidnapping

A power of butterfly must be
The aptitude to fly,
Meadows of majesty concedes
And easy sweeps of sky.

-Emily Dickinson

It isn't every day that you are asked if you are free to be kidnapped. Consent is oft-overlooked for kidnappers. The presence of it was not lost on young Russ.

Russ's attitude flipped from concern about the situation to curiosity to see how far he could take it. It is not every day that the man known throughout the entire community as the leader of the potato heads *asks* if he can kidnap you. Although a strained relationship, his parents knew Hubba.

Russ was calm and collected in his response. He knew that he was safe-ish, but had questions.

"What's the plan?" Russ asked.

"I don't really have a plan, Sparky told me to take and terrorize you, so probably some of that," Hubba said.

"Yeah, hard pass, but thank you for the consideration," Russ offered.

Hubba replied, "Hmm, I get it, what if we drive around? I have the corporate credit card. I could buy you stuff."

Russ grinned, "Yeah, that sounds much better... sure, I think that would be fine, let me just check with my parents and make sure that they are okay with it. Can you give me five minutes?"

Hubba said, "Five minutes, no problem, I can just wait here for you."

Russ floated inside with a huge smile on his face. He was beaming. He came in and sat down next to his father Owyhee Kenny. He was *still* recovering from the tractor injury. Russ just sat down and waited for his father to ask about why he was smiling so big? Finally, Owyhee Kenny noticed and said, "What? Are you going to tell me why you have that ridiculous look on your face?" Russ wanted to wait a little longer before he shared everything. He thought that the situation was funny. He waved his hand a bit with a stupid grin until his father finally broke down and said, "WHAT? WHAT IS THE STUPID GRIN?"

Finally, Russ and shared, "The leader of the potato heads are outside and he just *asked* if he could kidnap me. I told him that I was going to come inside and check in with my parents to make sure that they were OK with it. So, can I get kidnapped by the head of the potato heads?"

Owyhee Kenny started to laugh as well and said, "There is no way that I am going to let you get into the car with that man."

"Dad, the dude doesn't want to do this. You don't ask someone if they want to be kidnapped, you don't offer to buy them stuff, you just take them. You don't let them go inside and ask permission from their parents. As strange as it sounds, I feel bad for the guy and kind of want to see where this goes. I will take a lot of pictures," Russ responded.

"Let me talk to him, you're right, it does sound suspiciously peculiar. If after talking to him, I agree that he is harmless you can be kidnapped. I will send you with the cell phone, and if anything at all goes weird, you will call me right away."

Russ smiled and nodded.

Owyhee Kenny hobbled outside and waved at Hubba. Hubba jumped out of his car and ran over to Owyhee Kenny.

Owyhee Kenny began, "So you are interested in kidnapping my son?" Hubba, as though he was responding to the father of his prom date said, "Yes sir."

Owyhee Kenny followed up with "And when he will be home?" Hubba sheepishly responded, "Before Midnight... sir"

"Have a great time," Owyhee Kenny said as he turned and walked away.

Russ ran out to see Hubba and said, "Great news, my dad said that you can kidnap me."

Because of the sleep deprivation, and the pressure resting his shoulders, Hubba felt like this was a HUGE victory. He yelled at Russ, "Hop in," gesturing at the car.

The idea of kidnapping was absurd. This is not what normal, sane people do. Despite that, Russ felt safe and was interested in seeing what would happen that day. At best, the plan was disjointed for Hubba, at worst it was criminal.

They both hopped in the car. Hubba turned the car on and started to drive. After about five minutes of driving, Russ said, "You know, I have never been kidnapped before, I have no idea what to expect, can you give me a game plan on what to expect? Should I get in the trunk? I can."

Hubba responded, "Look, I don't know either, I have never kidnapped before either. If I need you to get in the trunk, we can do that later."

Russ promptly replied, "I want to get custom T-shirts made that say 'Kidnapper' and 'Kidnappee.'"

To state his case even more plainly, Russ said with a smile on his face, "I want a T-shirt or I will scream, **Help police! I just got kidnapped**."

Hubba thought about it for a moment and realized that he was deep into this little fiasco. He was confused and still trying to collect his own thoughts. Shirts seemed like a terrible idea.

It did keep the kid happy, so he might as well get the shirts made. They stopped at one of those custom shirt shops and had two shirts made.

Russ immediately put his kidnappee shirt on and encouraged Hubba to do the same. At first, Hubba was hesitant to put his shirt on but eventually buckled under the pressure. Both of them, sitting there in the car wearing kidnapper and kidnappee shirts.

He grabbed Hubba and yelled "Selfie TIME!" He leaned in close to Hubba and took their picture, t-shirts in full view. Russ immediately sent the picture to his father in a text message that said, "See, everything is okay."

There was a moment that Russ was letting this just percolate. Finally he couldn't contain himself, and said, "I can't imagine being kidnapped by a better person."

Hubba grinned from ear to ear, looked Russ in the eye, and said, "Thank you for saying that, I am doing my best as a kidnapper, and frankly, it isn't easy."

"Can we stop and get some Gatorade at the next kwik-e-mart?" Russ asked. This was both because he was thirsty and because he wanted to parade around in his new custom t-shirt. Hubba responded, "You know, I am thirsty too, let's do it!"

They pulled up to a kwik-e-mart, where they both hopped out of the car. Hubba was desperate for caffeine. Russ was curious to see how far he push the situation. When they got into the store, Russ said from two aisles over, "Hey kidnapper, can I get peanut butter

116

pretzels? You know pretzels with peanut butter inside of them."

Hubba, at first, only partially aware that he was just called kidnapper in the kwik-e-mart said, "Yeah, get two bags, one for me, and you don't have to call me kidnapper, you can call me Hubba."

Russ replied, "Got it, two bags, and if it's all the same, I would like to keep the roles clear so that there aren't any surprises. What if I accidentally switched roles and tried to kidnap you, chaos, think about it."

Hubba was a smart enough man. His childhood was that of working a potato farm. His grades were fine, and he graduated from high school. He didn't go on for any additional education. He wasn't dumb. He was piled high with stress, anxiety, and exhaustion. Advocates of torture will tell you that this is a time when you are most suggestible.

"I will just keep calling you kidnapper, and you can call me victim, kidnappee or how about just hostage. It just keeps the roles clear."

Hubba, taken aback, said "Okay, victim??? It just doesn't sound right." Russ, said, "Listen, you kidnapped me. I think that it is only fair to recognize the effort." And again, Hubba went along with it.

The two of them had progressed up to the checkout line. The cashier had heard most of the conversation but was a bit confused, so when he looked at Russ and said, "that will be $7.32," he didn't know what to expect. Was this a real kidnapping situation? There were no Amber Alerts, and the young man seemed to be agreeable to the whole situation.

Russ jumped in and said. "My kidnapper is going to pay for this." Hubba was starting to be aware that there were other people listening. Something that normally he would have been acutely aware of but today was oblivious for the previously stated reasons.

Hubba pulled out his debit card, and said, "Kidnapper may not be the exact right word. I stopped by his house this morning because my boss told me I had to disappear the kid." At this point, the transaction was completed. Hubba was given a receipt, which he catalogued. The cashier thanked him for his business and they walked back out to the car and he kept driving.

Hubba, drinking the largest cup of coffee from a gas station that any man should consume and Russ drinking Gatorade, both eating Peanut Butter Pretzels. The two of them sat there while driving around in circles on the street grid of a very small town.

Until finally, Russ asked, "What is our plan? Where are we going?"

"I don't know. I haven't ever kidnapped anyone before. What should we do?" Hubba replied.

Honestly, Russ didn't know how to respond. He didn't have a plan either. He was in it for the adventure and a teensy-bit of mockery. He entered into a moment where he started to empathize a bit with Hubba. He started to realize the amount of pressure that Hubba was under to try to do something like this.

The pressure didn't make the situation okay. It just made Hubba seem more human.

Russ thought about it and then proposed his idea. "It may sound weird, but there are these Japanese Internment Camps from World War II era that I would really like to see. I know that it is a bit gloomy, but I had a friend tell me about these, and I would really, really like to see them. There is one east on the interstate, past Twin Falls in a little place called Minidoka."

Twin Falls, Idaho, or Twin, as the locals called it, was about two hours from Blackfoot. It is a city steeped in irony. There is not much to know about the city of Twin Falls. No one famous has ever come from Twin, except the character "99" from the 1960s television show "Get Smart."

As for the geography of the region. There are three waterfalls, not two. They are Pillar Falls, Twin Falls, the town's namesake, and the grandest, the most notable and most photographed, Shoshone Falls.

Just West of Twin Falls is Minidoka National Park. It is literally where the country roads end.

And, in a final downpour of irony, the former Japanese-American residents who had owned, business and were homeowners had been told that they had to relocate East of the Washington/Idaho border. If they didn't relocate, they were rounded up and taken to Minidoka, or places like it, where they were watched, and treated like prisoners, guard towers and all. Russ' story was converging with his counselor, Ms. Yamada.

Minidoka is a National Historic Site, run by the National Parks.

Park, a word often reserved for places that contain merry-go-rounds, slides, and climbing walls. In this case, the park was a somber destination for travelers.

It is a place of recreation with walking trails and very nice signs commemorating aspects of the internment camp. The Signs would indicate where the barracks had stood, the food hall, the garden. A guide to help visitors understand what life was like in this unfortunate part of American History.

There is a very large sign at the entrance of the park that listed residents of this internment camp that opted to serve in the United State Military. People were defending the country that had locked them up for their ethnic background.

Minidoka is no longer a place of great fear and ignorance. It is now just a name on a map, with a few dilapidated buildings remaining and some walking trails. It is a place for Americans to remember, and a place standing as a beacon for the country to never unleash those atrocities again.

Russ wanted to go to Minidoka, something inside him was beckoning him there.

Hubba was a bit confused and asked "Why do you want to go to Minidoka" A place that Hubba had learned about in elementary school as a footnote in his Idaho State History course. "Isn't that the Japanese internment camp from World War II? There is nothing out there, it is a barren wasteland."

Russ was beginning to trust Hubba a little bit and was even beginning to like him. So he felt comfortable sharing, "Well, I was spending time with my guidance counselor from School, you met her, she is a Japanese-American. Her family moved to Idaho because of World War II, because they were Japanese. Ms. Yamada was telling me about what it is like to live in the midst of tension or pressure. You may or may not know this but we are probably going to lose our potato farm because we aren't making enough money. My father nearly killed from an unexplained tractor accident. We don't have savings, we don't have a plan and with that, there is a sense of tension. The same tension that Ms. Yamada's family felt when they moved to Idaho, the same tension that Ms. Yamada feels every day. So, I kinda think that going to Minidoka might help me understand that tension a little bit more. I don't know what I will see or hear, or smell. But at some level, I think being there will help me understand this place in life that I'm in."

Hubba heard every word, and with each word, each syllable he felt more and more responsible. As Hubba was getting more and more confused, Russ was understanding his own situation more and more.

Halfway between boy and man. Halfway between potato farmer and not. Russ was learning to live with the tension of real life. He was now heading to Minidoka, both on the Interstate highway with his kidnapper and was headed toward a figurative one. He was starting to understand the new normal in life that Ms. Yamada had told him about.

Instead of tricking Hubba into sending a

message to his dad, now Russ asked, "I know that my dad may be worried, can I send him a message and let him know what we are doing?"

Hubba thought that the text message was a good idea.

The more time that they spent together, the more that they were both changing on the inside.

As they drove those two hours, Russ continued to share his life, his thoughts, his perspective with his kidnapper and Hubba listened.

Hubba was reflecting on his own life and his own choices and understanding his own situation as well. He was loyal to Sparky, there was an oath, a private contract that Hubba took in his heart the day that his mother was symptom-free of cancer. Sparky had redirected SIPC funds to buy Hubba's family's farm freeing up the resources needed for treatment.

He committed that he would do whatever it took to help take care of Sparky. That decision that he made in his youth had long and impacting consequences. For Hubba, one of those consequences was that he had just committed a federal crime. He kidnapped a kid that he could absolutely relate to and generally liked.

As the two of them pulled into the Minidoka National Historic Site, Hubba uttered that he was sorry. Now Russ thought that Hubba was sorry for kidnapping him and at some level that was true.

But Hubba meant a lot more.

He was sorry for his SIPC involvement.

He was sorry for leading the Potato Heads.

He was sorry for scaring Russ's family.

He was sorry for the tractor accident.

He was sorry for stealing potato farms.

He was sorry for Everything.

The kidnapping was too far. Hubba's time with Russ and his sheer exhaustion had shown a spotlight on that fact. It was this point, where Hubba's allegiance shifted to Owyhee Kenny and the farmers of Blackfoot.

People can change. The person that we are today is not the person that we have to be tomorrow. For both Hubba and Russ, they were changing. Neither man wanted to be the same person that they were, both men wanted to be better, to be different.

They got out of the car, wearing their kidnapper/kidnappee shirts. They walked slowly taking it all in. They even took pictures, still in their t-shirts.

The rundown dormitory-style buildings that previously housed Japanese-Americans against their will were now the centerpiece of their photos. Most of the building had fallen down or were torn down. Those that were left would have Russ kneeling in front of them with a toothy smile on his face.

A guard tower had been rebuilt so that tourists could understand this was no summer camp. These were prisoners. Hubba had his picture taken at this locale, smiling.

There were also informative signs that pointed at where buildings used to be. Few remnants of structures remained serving as scars on the land for what had happened here.

They stopped and photographed read each sign.

Hubba and Russ still had scars too. Change means that there is a new normal. It doesn't mean that the past disappears. For Hubba, the scars would mandate that he make reparations to those he had wronged, as an atonement for his past.

At this point, both men were so entranced by this name on a map. They had forgotten that they were wearing their shirts altogether. This moment for both men was their Chrysalis each was changing. There were silent contracts made that day.

The two men got back into the car for the long drive home. On the way to Minidoka there was a lot of talking. The return trip had solemn awareness of where they had come from and where they were going. Hubba drove under the speed limit. There was no radio, just raindrops on the windshield and the rhythmic sound of the squeak of the windshield wipers. Their pilgrimage back to Blackfoot was near over.

Hubba pulled up to the potato farm and said "Thank you for letting me kidnap you today. This was probably one of the most meaningful days of my life."

PRO TIP: Replace your windshield wipers, it isn't just for you, but for the people who ride with you.

Russ responded, "Surprisingly, this was also a huge day for me. Thank you for having the courage to kidnap me." Which may go down as one of the strangest conversations ever in both men's lives.

Russ walked into his house, greeted his father who had a lot of questions. Russ shared what they had done that day. He shared that even though Hubba had attempted to kidnap, he felt sorry for the man.

Russ was tired from a long day. He went to bed. Despite being exhausted, the same was not true for Hubba.

Great!

*Something has happened, hasn't it? ... It's
like being up close to something so large you
don't even see it. Even now, I'm not sure I
can. But I know it's there.*

— *Ian McEwan*

After a full day of kidnapping, Hubba was
confused and *exhausted.* He had to recover from
the most traumatic event of his life, kidnapping
a minor.

Cycling the same pattern of streets over
and over again, around and around. He was
driving a loop. Thoughts were betraying him.
Ideas and beliefs that had always held true were
put into doubt. Up was down. Left was right. In
his mind, he would trace an argument to its
logical conclusion. Each time he thought that he

had reached a stopping point, the recorder in his head started to replay. It would counter all of the progress that he had made and the thought loop restarted.

Things had to be made right with Owyhee Kenny. He knew there were things that needed to be said and amends that needed to be made.

Hubba's car ended up in front of the Ibaiguren family farm yet again. He had been here so many times before. There were tire ruts worn into the earth from the potato head cars. Hubba's tires slid right into the worn grooves.

He noticed the ruts. His thoughts betrayed him. He could envision his trial and a Johnny Cochran-like attorney grandstanding with the phrase, "If the ruts fit, commit!"

Before the tractor accident, the Potato Heads were regular visitors to the farm. They were always across the street, always watching. Since the accident, there was no evidence of the SIPC other than the worn ruts, the enormous dinosaur, and the work that had been done on the new swimming pool.

It was late and Hubba was tired. This visit felt different despite the eerie resemblance to previous ones. This time, Hubba came to the farm as a visitor.

Hubba humbly walked across the street fully aware of his malfeasances. He also knew that he was visiting the father of the son that he had just kidnapped.

He had no false pretense that his apology would remedy the broken relationship.

Ironically, there was a massive metal Tyrannosaurus Rex blocking the front door. It had not yet been moved poolside. The potatoes had rotted, and all that was left was this giant dinosaur.

Ironically Hubba, while seeking atonement, could not reach the doorbell because of Cretaceous-era metal beast.

With some uncomfortable stretching, his pointer finger extended, found the glowing button and applied just enough pressure to connect the electrical circuit. This sound prompted Owyhee Kenny to hobble to the door.

Hubba stood there watching the doorknob turn. The door opened and Owyhee Kenny was standing there. It was humbling to see the man that he had wronged. Hubba believed he had a part in wrecking the tractor, kidnapping his son and ultimately stealing his farm.

After staring at each other in disbelief for what seemed like an eternity, Hubba broke the silence. "Owyhee Kenny, we have known each other for a long time, and it has been a long time since we knew each other well."

Owyhee Kenny interrupted, "I think that I know where this is going. Can we get out of here, get some food and a drink? I have been stuck in this house for so long. You will have to drive. We will have to use the back door, because, T-Rex"

Hubba, taken aback responded, "Sure, we can go somewhere, this late, where?" It was ten o'clock.

"River's Edge!"

This was a rafting themed bar and restaurant.

One wall of the restaurant was river routes

128

through Southeast Idaho.

One wall was pictures of rafters.

One wall was the kitchen.

The last wall was curiously dedicated to rafting deaths on the river.

The two men hobbled in and after being greeted at the door were whisked to their table adjacent to the wall of river deaths.

Once settled at the table, Hubba piped up where he had left off previously, "I came here to apologize. I have made many mistakes."

An overly chipper voice interrupted, "Hi my name is RJ and I will be you river-guide this evening. Is this your first time here?"

The server dressed in a life preserver, shorts, fanny pack, and river-sandals. Right behind him was a mousey little woman, dressed identically, did a half-wave with her right hand and said, "My name is Carole, and I am in training."

Both men nodded.

RJ handed Owyhee Kenny two broken paddles with the menu printed on it. Carol handed them identical menus. He continued, "Welcome to River's Edge, the only rafting-themed restaurant in Southeast Idaho. Can I start you with somcthing to drink?"

Carole, who was in training jumped in, "Welcome to River's Edge, Can I also start you with something to drink?"

Holding four paddles, Owyhee Kenny looked at RJ and then Carole and said, "How about a couple of pints?"

RJ responded, "Yes, what would you like?"

Carole added, "Yes, what would you like?"

Owyhee Kenny said, "Betta-Cola please."

Hubba followed with, "Rafter's Blonde"

RJ said "Great!" and darted away, Carole in tote, her foot echoing everyone of his footsteps.

Hubba looked at Owyhee Kenny and continued, "Like I was saying, I came here to apologize."

Owyhee Kenny, puzzled, said, "She didn't say 'great'. She copied everything that RJ said except the word 'great'."

Still trying, Hubba said, "I have done a lot of bad things, some against you and some against your family"

"Alright, here are two pints of-of our Rafter's Blond," said RJ and he placed the glasses down.

Right behind him, Carole placed two glasses in front of Hubba and said, "Alright, here are two pints of our Betta-Cola."

And the two servers disappeared as quickly as they came.

Perplexed, but agreeable, Owyhee Kenny, took a drink and said, "That was weird, and this is smooth."

After nursing his drink for a bit, Hubba tried again, "Wow, I stopped by tonight to apologize, I have done horrible things to you and your family. Today when I drove your son, after having kidnapped, I realized that I"

RJ interrupted again, "Have you had a chance to look at the menu? Can I get you started with an appetizer?"

Carole echoed, "Have you had a chance to look at the menu? Can I get you started with an appetizer."

Owyhee Kenny picked up the menu paddle and said, "We will take an order of Rocky Mountain Oysters."

Hubba didn't know what Rocky Mountain Oysters were but was hungry, so he said, "Make it a triple order."

RJ asked, "Will there be anything else?"

Carole asked, "Will there be anything else?"

Owyhee Kenny replied, "I think that we are good, thank you."

RJ said, "Great," and the two disappeared again.

Hubba tried to continue, "Some of my offenses are against you and your family."

He was trying to listen to Hubba, but Owyhee Kenny interrupted, "She did it again, she didn't say 'great'. Why didn't she say great? Sorry Hubba, what were you saying?"

RJ carried one large plate of Rocky Mountain Oysters placed them on the table between the two men, and said, "Alright gentlemen, triple order, eat up. I hope that you have a ride home." He winked

Carole in tote carried a second triple order of Rocky Mountain oysters, placed them on the table and said, "Alright gentlemen, triple order, eat up, I hope that you have a ride home." She winked too.

"Can I get you anything else," RJ said.

"Can I get you anything else," Carole said.

Owyhee Kenny said, "No thank you, I think that we are good."

RJ said, "Great," and then the two servers

disappeared.

Owyhee Kenny said again, "She did it again! She didn't say 'great'. Go ahead and start on that appetizer, I mean, we have six orders"

Hubba still unaware what he was about to eat deep grabbed one, dipped it in a bowl of marinara and nearly swallowed it whole. He was very hungry. He ate five more.

"Slow down big fella, we have time. I have never seen anyone enjoy bull testicles this much."

Hubba responded, "These are bull testicles?" He was now aware of what he had eaten. He thought for a second and grabbed two more. Popping them in his mouth smirked and said, "Whatever, I'm hungry"

Owyhee Kenny said, "I thought that you knew what they were, you ordered a triple order, two actually"

His eyes clear as the day, Hubba said, "I don't know man, I came to apologize, I have done bad things, some against you, some against your family, some are against other people. This morning, I kidnapped your kin, a federal crime. I am pretty sure that we sabotaged your tractor, which led to your accident and for all of that I am sorry. And we are trying to steal your farm."

There was no doubt or disbelief that the person in front of Owyhee Kenny was sincere and not just pulling another scam for Sparky. He, himself was also a fallen man.

Owyhee Kenny was also fully aware that he had sabotaged his own tractor, creating the accident that was the catalytic event from which this all flowed down. He knew that he had lied, and was likely fraudulent in his health claim, as this was truly no accident. He had skeletons as well. You can appreciate another person's pain when you have experienced it yourself.

 PRO TIP: A firm handshake sets the tone for great conversations.

Owyhee Kenny said, "Hello, my name is Owyhee Kenny, we now know each other. It sounds like your trip today with my son had a profound impact on him and on you and for that, I am grateful. Hubba, you have made some bad choices in life, many that directly impact my family and me, but the truth is, so have I. I cannot in good conscience hold my grievances against you and expect other people to forgive me."

This is the message of the gospel. The message that they had heard, sitting in the Church listening to Pastor Skip's sermons. Hearing it in the church is very different than experiencing the opportunity to both forgive and be forgiven.

Hubba went on, "Listen, I want to do better, I can't make it right, but I can make it better. What can I do? How can I help your family recover from this miserable place that I have helped put you in?"

Owyhee Kenny thought about it, and said, "Actually, I have an idea." He opened his wallet and pulled out the business card for Kyle Pierce, the agent of the FPI. Owyhee Kenny handed him the card and said, "This gentleman stopped by my hospital room asking for details about Sparky and the SIPC. I was not in a position where I could share anything with the man, for both obvious and not so obvious reasons. So I took his card and it has been sitting in my wallet ever since. Listen, if you want to make things right with me and this community, give this man a call. Tell him what you have done and tell him what the SIPC is up to."

Hubba reached out and received the card with his right hand. He looked at the card, opened his wallet, and carefully filed it. "Listen, I will call the man and who knows maybe this can begin to make up for so many of the terrible things that I have done."

Owyhee Kenny extended his hand, Hubba cleaned his hand of Rocky Mountain Oyster grease and met Owyhee Kenny's.

Owyhee Kenny said, "I respect you for this. It isn't easy. I forgive you."

RJ appeared at the table, "Can I interest either of you in some dessert? We have a delicious taconut. It is our combination of a taco and donut. You can have Chocolate Peanut Butter, Strawberry Cheescake, or Graveyard. I don't recommend Graveyard. It is just a bunch of flavors mixed together."

Carole still following said, "Can I interest either of you in some dessert? We have a delicious taconut. It is our combination of a taco and donut. You can have Chocolate Peanut Butter, Strawberry Cheescake, or Graveyard. I don't recommend Graveyard. It is just a bunch of flavors mixed together."

Visibly shaken, both men holding back tears, looked at the wait staff and said, "That would be great"

RJ said, "Great" and disappeared with his mousey trainee.

RJ brought one graveyard taconut for both men, Carole brought one graveyard taconut for both men.

"Are you ready for a check?" RJ asked.

"Are you ready for a check?" Carole Asked.

"That would be great, just one is fine," Hubba said.

RJ reached into his fanny pack, and produced a check. Carole reached into her fanny pack and pulled out an identical check, both were handed to Hubba.

Owyhee Kenny took a bite of the graveyard taconut, "This is the worst desert, I have ever had, I think this is chocolate, creme fresh, oatmeal and chicken.

Hubba paid both checks, even leaving two tips, and they left.

He grabbed a comment card and wrote one word, "Great!"

Hubba drove Owyhee Kenny home. Then pulled in for one of those man-hugs and split ways. As Hubba walked back across the street that night, he was still fighting back tears.

Owyhee Kenny hobbled back to bed, also still reeling from what just took place.

Hubba did sleep that night. He slept well. He had been awake for 72 hours. Beyond that, it had been a long time since he had a "good" night's sleep. The next morning, he knew what he had to do. He had to call the number on the business card. The card that Owyhee Kenny had given him. While the concept of calling this "Kyle Pierce" person might seem easy enough, Hubba had to assume that someone was watching and listening. This reasonable paranoia meant that the mechanics of actually making that phone call were significantly more complicated than a normal person.

That morning, Hubba needed everything to look normal. He put on his bathrobe, and his slippers, a tradition that happened every Sunday.

He hopped in his car and drive to the local donut shop. There was a sign, that read, "Try the new Donaco, better than the Taconut! Part Taco, Part Donut." Hubba threw up in his mouth a little.

He purchased his normal order, exactly one apple fritter and one glazed donut. He would then go to the gas station next door where he would purchase a 42-ounce cup of coffee. The gas station was the only place that you could get that much coffee for a buck. While he was there, Hubba purchased a burner phone.

There were no secrets in Blackfoot, Idaho. If you controlled the cell towers, which the SIPC did, you could hijack voice calls and text messages. The potato heads knew about this level of scrutiny, so anytime you needed to make a call, you could, but you had to be careful. The easiest solution was to use a burner phone. A burner phone uses a phone that has a prepaid sim card. The first time a burner phone is used, some level of anonymity can be assumed. After that, all bets for privacy were off.

Hubba drove outside of town far enough to purchase the phone, where he was out of range from the watchful eyes of the SIPC.

Hubba had no idea what the outcome of the call was going to be. He knew that he needed to make things right. Somehow, this person, this call, felt like the way that he could make some of his amends.

The name on the card read "Kyle Pierce." The address was Salt Lake City, Utah. Idaho and Utah are side by side. Blackfoot is about a three-hour drive from Salt Lake City. The word "barren" effectively describes the wasteland of mile after mile of emptiness.

One aspect of living in Blackfoot meant that you were being watched; Hubba knew this. He knew that Sparky was so deranged that he would not just assign a potato head to follow someone. He would assign a potato head to follow the already-following potato head. Because of this persistent surveillance, Hubba knew he had to be one step ahead.

Hubba's best chance for avoiding the situation was for the call to go straight to Voicemail, which he secretly wanted.

Unfortunately, or fortunately for Hubba, after dialing, a voice on the other end of the phone, broke the ring, and said, "Federal Potato Investigators, this is Kyle Pierce."

Staring at a Hole

No person shall be held to answer for a capital, or otherwise infamous crime, unless on a presentment or indictment of a grand jury, except in cases arising in the land or naval forces, or in the militia, when in actual service in time of war or public danger; nor shall any person be subject for the same offense to be twice put in jeopardy of life or limb; nor shall be compelled in any criminal case to be a witness against himself, nor be deprived of life, liberty, or property, without due process of law; nor shall private property be taken for public use, without just compensation.

-   Fifth Amendment of the US Constitution

Ill-preparedness was emerging as a theme for Hubba. He had no plan for the phone call with the Federal Agent.

Some examples of a plan might be to confess to everything, deny every last detail or trade information for leniency. Do not meet a federal agent when you are guilty, and lack a plan.

Hubba was a yard sale. It felt like his whole life for sale on the front lawn. His highest hope was to win roommate roulette in federal prison.

The Fifth Amendment of the Constitution protects US citizens from incriminating themselves. Hubba did not understand the constitution.

 PRO TIP: Exchange information to the federal police in exchange for shorter prison terms.

"Hello, my name is Hubba. I work with the Southeast Idaho Potato Council." Hubba paused, and waited, mostly to make sure that the person on the other end of the phone was listening and not a wrong number.

"Hi Hubba, thank you for calling, how did you get this number?" Kyle Pierce asked.

"Well, it is a long story, but I kidnapped Owyhee Kenny's son, Russ Ibaiguren, who is a great kid. He and I drove about twelve hours through Idaho, and in the process of kidnapping the kid, I realized that in my life, all of the things that I have done for the Southeast Idaho Potato Council have been rotten. Last night after I realized the error in my ways and I returned Russ back to his family, I went back over to

Owyhee Kenny's house and apologized for everything. He gave me your card and suggested that I give you a call," Hubba rambled in a single breath.

Kyle Pierce responded in a much slower, methodical tone, "Well, I am glad that you called, I know your case very well. Frankly, I have not been able to get any information about anything from that district."

Kyle Pierce paused, and then added, "Kidnapping is always wrong but, it is good that you changed your mind. We have a little saying here at the FPI, 'Kidnapping is never the right choice.'"

Normally kidnapping is a major offense, but it went unreported. Additionally, Kyle Pierce worked for the United States Department of Agriculture and had no idea how to handle a kidnapping other than call 911 himself.

He continued, "Your community is locked up tight. I would like to talk to you, but can't make it to Blackfoot until late this week. Would that timeframe work for you?"

"I don't want you to come here," Hubba said, "It isn't safe. The reason that no one will talk to you is that the SIPC, Big Potato, is always watching and always listening, everywhere. The only way that I could call you today was by purchasing a burner phone at the Kwik-e-Mart. I think a better plan would be for me to come to Salt Lake. Can I come today? I will make the four-hour drive take eight hours.

Let's meet at the Bear River Migratory Bird Refuge, I will pull up in a late model off-brand imported blue sports car.

"I will meet you there in eight hours," Kyle Pierce agreed.

Camera, phone, and keys are all that Hubba grabbed, and true to form, within 5 minutes of the drive, there was a car following him.

It was one of the Potato Heads, no one was off limits. This was the paranoia that Sparky had inspired. The Potato Head's name was Dirk, he was assigned to "ad-hoc" henchman. He could do whatever he wanted to whomever he wanted. After a short time, he realized he was following his own boss. He continued as he thought that it would be received as him unwavering in his commitment to his job.

There are two ways to evade a follower: First, you can outrun them. You create a high-speed chase. This approach will always draw suspicion.

The other option was to bore them to death: drive slow; stop a lot; take a lot of pictures. This was the opposite of a high-speed chase, it was low-speed.

The drive was slow. Dirk was trying to stay awake, and remain unseen while traveling half the speed limit on the freeway.

GET TO KNOW IDAHO: Idaho law forbids a citizen to give another citizen a box of candy that weighs more than 50 pounds.

Dirk followed Hubba everywhere. They stopped in Mountain Home at a mural made entirely out of pennies. They stopped at the fuel stop in Sublett on the state line. It was a mix between a petting zoo, gas station and tourist trap. Hubba took a picture of each animal there, and yes, he, himself was bored.

It was at this point that Dirk decided his harassment would be better placed on anyone or anything else. Dirk wrote in his harassment journal, "Torn between staring at a hole in the ground and this guy, I would choose the hole. The only time he has something interesting to say is when Pentecost and Easter are on the same day. He would have left the circus to become an accountant. It would be better to watch paint dry or the grass grow. He is a stale, stuffy, stodgy stoicist, The dude is the dullest, boring person in the entire world."

And it was at this point that Hubba was free to go about his business.

The state line between Idaho and Utah is not very noteworthy. It has a sign that says "Welcome to Utah, the Beehive state."

As Hubba drove down the interstate, the majesty of the Rocky Mountains loomed in their grandeur. Snow speckling the peaks with accumulations at the top, and snow fading down to nothingness. The jagged peaks co-mingling with the snow revealing deeply jaded craigs. On the other side of the car, streams and pools of water started to form into the Great Salt Lake. The Great Salt Lake is the largest body of water west of the Mississippi River and ten times saltier than ocean water.

As Hubba grew closer to the Bird Refuge, his heart was pounding, his pupils were dilated. He was in an acute state of awareness.

His car made its final turn. The long lush grasslands contained an entire ecosystem of species. Stunningly beautiful in every direction. This is where the mountain meets the water. Ironically, the kind of place you might want to stop and take pictures.

Unfortunately, the irony of the picturesque landscape was lost completely on Hubba, and not a single photo of it was taken.

The temperature outside was dropping because it was late fall. This time of year, there are two temperatures at the Bear River Migratory Bird Refuge, frozen, and tundra. Despite the weather, the refuge was still abuzz with activity.

For a split second, Hubba was captivated and forgot everything going on in his life. For a moment, he forgot that he was ultimately coming to meet with a Federal Agent.

The place was captivating, there were birds everywhere. Some feasting on brine shrimp. As Hubba wandered down the trail, soaking in the wildlife. There were swallows and sparrows, swans and shrikes. There were gnatcatchers and warblers.

"Mr. Potato Head, I presume," Officer Pierce guessed. "It is great to meet the great Mr. Potato Head."

Hubba was quick to respond, "I am done with that. Yesterday, I kidnapped a minor. I drove here to turn myself in. Lock me up, man, I will confess to everything." Officer Pierce studied Hubba until finally stating, "You know I work for the Federal Potato Investigators, a division of the *United States Department of Agriculture.* I only have jurisdiction to arrest you in matters relating to crimes associated with Potatoes."

"But I kidnapped a minor," Hubba said,

The FPI agent responded, "Were there undersized potatoes in your pocket and was the kidnapping reported to the authorities? If the answer is no to either of the questions, then, No, I cannot arrest you"

He continued, "Hubba, I know you have done dreadful things, but you have been following orders, I don't care about you, I care about the one calling the shots. I want to cut the head of the snake off. You are not the head, Sparky is"

"What do you need to get to Sparky?" Hubba asked.

"I need evidence, a lot of evidence. I need testimonials, I need records, phone conversations and I need things that show that Sparky plays outside the rules and that that directly impacts potato farming."

Hubba's eyes narrowed, he was listening.

Officer Pierce continued, "At the end of the day, I have to show the connection between potatoes and corruption. Maps, documents, and honestly, what we really need is a recorded confession. Can you get me a recorded confession?"

Officer Pierce was asking Hubba to put his own life at risk to get Sparky to incriminate himself.

Hubba let out a deep sigh, "You know, twenty-four hours ago, I would have spit in your face, and walked away. But today, I think that the answer *is* yes. What are the details? Do I need to wear a wire? I want a safe word, so that when I say the word "cacophony" you swoop in with military-grade Apache helicopters, tanks, whatever firepower you have, and pull me out of there. It might be overkill, but I know this man far too well." Hubba gestured overhead pointing at the helicopters that weren't there.

Officer Pierce waited for Hubba to finish and then said, "We don't have any of that. We don't have helicopters, we don't have tanks, we don't have any firepower, it is a fact that only a few FPI agents even have vehicles allocated to them. When I say vehicles, you should think pickup with non-functioning AM radios. So, there will be no cover fire for safe words. In fact, I have worse news. We are the FPI, we don't even have wires, just record the conversation on your cell phone. Idaho is a one-party recording state. You don't even need permission to record him. You just have to do it."

Hubba thought about it, and finally responded, "I'll do it, I don't know how, but I will record him incriminating himself."

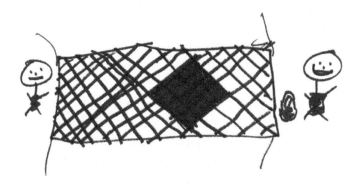

Sweet Potatopia

*It does not do to leave a live dragon out of
your calculations if you live near him.*
    -        *J.R.R Tolkien, The Hobbit*

In the marshland, a lone kingfisher bent over. It
thrust his beak into the watery marsh and pulls
out a grouper. The moment caught the eye of
both men and almost seemed like a sign from
the cosmos that this conversation was
sanctioned and commissioned.

They shook hands and parted.

Hubba got into his car and drove home.
He went faster on the return trip. He was pretty
occupied with how he was going to convince
Sparky to incriminate himself. As he drove, he
mulled over the different ideas of how to get
Sparky to talk. Granted, he had four hours in
the car and it was already getting late.

So many years ago, when Sparky and
Hubba first met, they were friends, out of
convenience. Part of the friendship was the

146

geography of the community. The next family with children Hubba's age were a couple of farms away. So you played with who was there regardless of what you had in common with them.

Sparky didn't start out the farm-stealing archetypal villain that he is today. His parents moved to Blackfoot to plant sweet potatoes and failed miserably. The only people that would take them in was Hubba's family.

Then one abysmal month, Hubba's mother fell victim to breast cancer. Cancer is a prison sentence, sometimes a life sentence. It is the great equalizer. It does not discriminate, it strikes rich and poor, tall and short and men and women. You can never be prepared for cancer. You go to the doctor complaining about a lump or a mild pain and you leave forever changed. You can have the greatest health insurance in the world, and cancer will break you down, and leave you a huddled mass in the corner.

Hubba's family had no financial cushion. Like all potato farmers in the area, they were already living hand to mouth, and the diagnosis was grim.

Sparky volunteered with the SIPC and as part of his regular routine. He went to the bank to deposit more checks. It was like clockwork. One deposit, he pushed an envelope full of checks across the table to a woman in a blue dress. As she was counting the checks, she said, "I heard about the farm, it's a real shame. You know that they only owe $80,000 on the farm, that isn't very much." To which Sparky replied,

"No? It seems like a lot, where are they gonna find that kind of scratch? $80,000? They don't have it." To which the lady in blue replied, "There is $78,213 in the SIPC account. With these deposits, you should be very close to being able to buy the farm."

His stomach turned with excitement, Sparky knew that with this money he could help Hubba's family farm survive. He reached out to the director of the SIPC with the idea. "We could purchase the farm and create a consistent revenue stream for the SIPC. We will still need to collect dues, but we could establish a fund that helps local potato farmers."

The original request was altruistic, but for Sparky, it unlocked the ability to buy and sell people, ideas, and things. And, he could do it through manipulation and with other people's money. This was about leverage and control. If he could save Hubba's mother, he would control their family.

It was settled, the director of the SIPC reached out to Hubba's family. He proposed the idea that they would sell the family farm to the SIPC and Hubba and Sparky's family would continue to live on and work the farm. They could repurchase the farm if they were ever in position to do so. Sparky's relationship with Hubba forever changed that day.

The fact that Sparky helped save Hubba's mother so many years ago weighed heavy on Hubba about his betrayal.

He knew that if he went to the SIPC office the next day, Sparky would be all business and wouldn't share a thing. He kept thinking that if stopped at Sparky's house, that may put him at ease. And suddenly Hubba had a plan!

When Hubba returned to Blackfoot, he made two stops on the way to Sparky's house.

First, he stopped by his own house, opened his secure, looming safe and grabbed a very large sum of money, all of it and placed it in a nondescript duffle bag. Hubba had never trusted banks, or at least not after the family farm incident.

As a single man, he has never had large expenses so he had accumulated a large sum of cash. In total Hubba grabbed about $100,000 in large bills. He knew that he had questions to ask and needed answers, and the only way to get those answers was to make a strong outward sign. One that he was serious. He had to buy answers. Cash will do that.

 LIFE TIP: Get a savings account at a bank and put money in it. It should be triple times your monthly income.

For Sparky and the SIPC, one hundred thousand dollars was not "Screw you" money. "Screw you" money is enough that you can look at your employer and say, "screw you." This money was enough for Sparky to take notice and believe that Hubba was serious.

The second stop was the liquor store. He purchased a very nice, expensive bottle of vodka that he could bring and share with Sparky. Alcohol often lubricates communication channels and gets people to say things that they might not say in a non-impaired state.

This was a technique that he had used several times when working with potato farmers as a potato head. Also, Hubba was freaked out by what he was about to do. He knew that he was about to upheave one of the longest relationships in his life, so a little bit of personal vodka would go a long way in terms of building his confidence.

He double-checked his phone to make sure that he had enough battery power and available memory to be able to record the entire time with Sparky. He pulled into the driveway. There were three Cairns stacked up right outside of Sparky's house. Cairns that were not built by Sparky, but that just appeared. Several times, Sparky has disassembled them and several times the Cairns just reappeared.

When Hubba arrived at Sparky's house, he set his phone to record. He took a deep breath, grabbed the vodka and the duffle of cash. He got out of his car, gently closing the door.

In Hubba's entire life, he had spent zero minutes at Sparky's house. He had never been invited, no one had. It was weird and yet it seemed right. No one questioned it, mostly because no one really wanted to be invited to his house.

After work hours, Sparky had always kept to himself. No one remembers after-dinner drinks or SIPC Softball League. Sparky always stayed later than anyone else and arrived earlier. Sparky only considered himself to have one friend, Hubba. Frankly, Sparky had never learned how to be someone's friend. This sounds like the kind of thing that everyone learns when they are little. But Sparky didn't. Although brilliant, he had the emotional intelligence of a four-year-old. Somehow, in spite of all his shortcomings, Hubba had still considered Sparky his friend.

Hubba understood his role in Sparky's life. He knew the damage that was about to be done in to this man. Yes, Hubba had other friends, but Sparky did not. This inequity weighed on Hubba. He also understood the damage that the SIPC and he himself had done. He knew that Sparky was the source of that damage, but it didn't make the betrayal any easier. There are no self-help books on how to betray "better." It comes down to sharpening your knives and stabbing in the direction of the person's back.

It was dark. There were no porch lights, no lights in the house. Hubba crept to the door and knocked at first very quietly and growing with intensity as he knocked more and more. Finally, Hubba, after his knuckles hurt from the pounding, was able to draw Sparky's attention.

Sparky came to the door. He looked through the peephole, as he was not used to company, ever. His eyes studied the dark figure.

In what would be the theme of the night, Hubba broke the silence. "Let me in. It is cold out here."

The door opened, and Sparky let Hubba in. The house smelled of garlic and despair. There were pieces of onion, garlic and cut pieces of sirloin, all near a little bottle of strychnine. Sparky had been working in the kitchen before

Hubba's arrival. There were still bits of steak cut thin on the counter and a pile of garlic cloves.

The book, "How The Farmer Can Save His Sweet Potatoes" by George Washington Carver, was still open on the table from where Sparky was reading it. The pages had been dog-eared and clearly used many times.

It was a bit weird for a single man to live in such a large house by himself. Hubba was prepared, being the perpetual Boy Scout that he was. He brought shot glasses. After both men sat down to the table, Hubba placed his cell phone down and poured two shots of vodka. There was one for each of them. Hubba pushed the vodka across the table. Both men grabbed their shots and drank them quickly. It was smooth, easy to have a second shot. Hubba poured the second round. As the two men took the glasses, Hubba looked at Sparky and said, "I want in."

Sparky, a bit surprised said, "Into what?"

"Into whatever you have going on. We have known each other for a long time, and I know that you don't just have a plan, you have a plan for after the plan, and a clean little master plan that ties them all together. I want in," Hubba replied.

This conversation was the type of the thing that Sparky was exceptional at deflecting, so he just smiled, and said, "Listen, once we lock up all of the potato farms in Blackfoot, we will just service the potato industry, we will contribute to the community and make sure that everyone has a part of what is going on. There is really nothing to be a part of."

Both men drank their second shot.

At this point, Hubba reached down to the floor and grabbed his duffle. It was an over the shoulder bag that is often misconstrued for a man purse. This was exactly Sparky's thought when he originally noticed the bag. Sparky smiled a short-lived crooked grin and Hubba continued, "In this bag, there is $100,000 cash. I want to ride shotgun. I want to buy a seat at the table. You have the Midas touch, everything that you touch turns to gold and I want a part of it. I don't want a free ride, I want a seat at the table, and I am hoping that $100,000 will buy that for me."

One hundred thousand dollars was not a lot of money to Sparky, but he understood that it was a lot of money to Hubba, so he looked at the money, smirked back at Hubba and said, "Fine, you're in."

Hubba poured another round of shots and said, "We should celebrate. Salut!"

The two men continued to drink, shot after shot. Slowly by slowly Sparky's inhibitions were disappearing and this was the beginning of the evidence. Hubba knew better than to ask direct and specific questions so early in the night. He was looking for many small "Yes" answers. He needed them one at a time. The first yes was allowing Hubba a seat at the table. Time passed and the two men spoke of times past.

And then it happened Sparky looked at Hubba and said, "Do you want to know what you got into?"

In his heart, Hubba knew that he had just set the hook and the rest of the night would be

153

dedicated to reeling this very large fish into the boat. Sparky was beginning to stride down a long path of incriminating himself. "Hubba, do you remember where I came from? Nashville, North Carolina. In Nashville, the sweet potato in the most important crop. My family moved to Blackfoot, to start a new life here and grow sweet potatoes. But no one would listen. Everyone was so sold on boring, plain potatoes, 'You can make tater tots' they would say. You can make flour, and fries, they would say.

Sweet potatoes are a god-given superfood. Eating sweet potatoes is like, taking steroids for your mind, body and." At this point, there was a bit of delay in Sparky's voice and then said "soul."

All of the key gestures one demonstrates to encourage the other person to continue talking were coming out of Hubba. He made eye contact and nodded his head along with everything that Sparky said. Because Sparky felt comfortable and was under full sail of vodka, he continued, "My parents gave everything to see their dream come true of growing sweet potatoes in Southeast Idaho, but no one cared. This is of course when we met. I liked you, I liked your family, but there was always this sense of failure that I felt for not doing more to get a sweet potato farm started."

Then Sparky started to smile. "What if I told you that I was going to rename the SIPC the Southeastern Idaho Sweet Potato Council? Everyone in this whole region will be growing sweet potatoes. Why? Because they don't have a choice. My parents' dream of growing sweet potatoes will finally come true. The only change is that the reign of stupid, boring, dumb potatoes are over. There is, of course, more. We are going to reinvest in the city. All of the garbage town-space that is there now will be replaced with new modern buildings each dedicated to an aspect of the sweet potato. There will be new roads and new opportunities. Hubba, we are going to have our own mascot, in PLUSH. We are going to have a theme park and roller coaster. On the roller coaster, each car will be a sweet potato painted on it."

At this point, Sparky's focus turned back to Hubba and he said, "And you bought your way into this. Hubba, we are going to make a gargantuan of money. A LOT."

Hubba was drunk-interested at this point and said, "How much money do you think we can make?" Sparky quickly responded, "at least 20x on your investment, but could be 40x if everything goes well."

Satisfied with the confession, he grabbed his mobile phone, and poured one more shot of vodka for both of them. They both grabbed the shot glasses, clinked and toasted to a very successful relationship.

"Do you want to see it?" Sparky said. "Do you want to see Sweet Potatopia? Follow me," and the two men descended into the panic room of all things sweet potato. As Hubba entered, he was greeted with a very large Sweet Potato plush toy dressed in Peruvian clothes. "You know sweet potatoes were discovered in Peru and then migrated to the Pacific islands, that is why the mascot is dressed Peruvian."

The room was dark and unkempt, a detail that was so out of place for Sparky. Hubba noticed the contrast, even in his intoxicated state. Every aspect of Sparky's life was organized and structured. He was a poster child for task lists. This organization is what has led to Sparky's drive and success. Which is why this other aspect of Sparky's life being chaotic was so notable.

As the two men continued through the labyrinth of maps and charts, Hubba was overwhelmed with what he saw. Every inch of the wall had papers tacked to it. There were pictures. There were maps. There were motivational phrases. There was even a calendar of events.

As they were nearing the very furthest edge, he saw a shrine dedicated to Owyhee Kenny and a large handwritten sign that read, "One more."

Hubba had a lot of thoughts, but no questions.

Standing in the lair of the beast, the novelty wore off for Hubba. The true nature of Sparky, a shallow empty man dedicated to one single thing, ruining the lives of potato farmers had become suffocating.

Hubba needed to go home. The only problem was that he was plowed, drunk. Sparky was too. Finally, Hubba mustered up the words to say, "I have to go home."

Sparky was so lit that he was unaware that Hubba was walking out of the house as drunk as he was. Hubba, on the other hand, had two goals: First, he wanted to get out of there as fast as he could. He had the confession on tape and was ready to go. Second, he had no interest in drunk sleeping at Sparky's house.

Hubba was facing a bit of a dilemma; he knew that he shouldn't be driving in his inebriated state. He got into his car and drove down the driveway out of view of the house. Hubba stopped the car, turned it off, and tipped his chair back. He slept off the "drunk." When he woke up the next morning, he felt like he was recovering from a barroom brawl.

Vodka drunk will do that to you.

He was concerned that he didn't remember what took place the night before. He decided to listen to the cell phone-recorded conversation. He reheard Sparky's pitch and was aware of just how much money he would stand to make. It was a lot and would be his if he just re-aligned himself with Sparky. After reflecting for some moments, Hubba was aware that he had not incriminated himself with Kyle Pierce, the FPI agent. Hubba did the math, 40 times on a $100,000 investment was $4,000,000 and for a kid who grew up on a potato farm, this was more money than he thought he would ever see in his lifetime.

Sitting in his car, a bit dumbfounded, Hubba was contemplating what he had just heard. He had the chance to make 40 times on his investment. The reality of that taking place was quite high because Sparky had proved that he could do what he said, over and over again.

Hubba was hung-over. The space between his ears felt like an echo chamber for his thoughts.

The details of what he had just heard were bouncing around inside his head. He truly could just suppress the evidence, assemble a bunch of non-incriminating stuff, and deliver that to the federal agent. The only reason he had to follow through on turning Sparky in was internal. And Hubba was thinking about it.

Forgiveness and Clearing the Air

Forgiveness is me giving up my right to hurt
you for hurting me. Forgiveness is the final
act of love. – Beyoncé

However, upon regaining his composure, Hubba turned his car on and drove to Owyhee Kenny's house before going home.

He wanted the visit to be quick. He ran to the door, with the phone in hand. As soon as Owyhee Kenny answered the door, Hubba exclaimed, "I did it, I got it, everything is right here." as he pointed at the phone.

Owyhee Kenny responded, "Did what, what is this?"

Hubba responded, that is Sparky

incriminating himself. Oh, and me giving Sparky my life savings. Hey, I have to run to work, but I wanted to let you know what was happening."

Owyhee Kenny teared up and went to hug Hubba. Hubba set the phone down to receive the embrace and drove home.

 LIFE TIP: The many benefits of forgiveness include lowered blood pressure and heart rate, decreased stress, less depression and anxiety, improved sleep, less pain and increased psychological well-being.

Hubba took a quick shower, and changed his clothes for work.

When he got out of the shower, he got dressed and poured himself a very, very tall cup of coffee. As he drank his life had more and more clarity. It wasn't about the money for him. It was never about the money.

When he drove Russ to Minidoka, he had tasted freedom. He wanted out of this cycle of shame. Showering didn't get him clean. He wanted a new life, a new existence, a new outlook. With each sip of his coffee, he was more and more composed and ready to bring down Sparky.

After finishing his cup, he looked around and saw a burner phone on the counter, and then another and another. He even brought a phone in from the car thinking that it was the original.

There was a phone on the coffee table, two next to the big fluffy chair. There were a lot of burner phones, and Hubba had no idea where he put his down when he came in. Hubba was a bachelor. That means that he did not have anyone living with him. He didn't clean up after himself except for when it was really important. He would often joke with the other potato heads that he would clean his apartment when the President would come for dinner.

The "Clean for the President" approach was starting to show some holes. There were literally 100 identical burner phones, all without charge. Every time Hubba needed to make a private call, he would run down to the Kwik-e-mart and purchase another burner phone. He would make his one call and then discard the phone somewhere in his apartment. It was clear that this was going to be a bigger problem for him than he had originally thought.

He collected all the phones and had 102 in total. Ironically, in order for him to call the FPI agent, Kyle Pierce, he needed to get at least one more burner phone.

Hubba went out to his car and drove to the Kwik-e-mart where he would purchase one more phone to call Officer Pierce. He needed to figure out a plan on how to give the officer so many phones. As Hubba was driving, he realized another problem, he had just given Sparky, 100,000 dollars. He knew that Sparky was going to keep a record of this money. There was a ledger and his name was on it. 100,000 dollars was a gateway to great wealth if Sparky got away with it. However, if he didn't, the only evidence in the entire world that protected Hubba from the FPI was contained on one of these uncharged burner phones. This paradoxical reality weighed heavy on him.

He purchased another burner phone from the Kwik-e-mart. This phone looked exactly like every other phone that he had purchased previously. It was the same model, the same shop, the same cost. The phone was identical.

Hubba got back into his car and drove home to make the phone call. He pulled out Officer Pierce's business card again. This time when he dialed the phone, the numbers seemed easier to press. The phone started to ring and Officer Pierce answered it immediately. "Kyle Pierce, Federal Potato Investigator."

"Listen, I know who you are," Hubba said. He continued, "I got the recording. I was able to get Sparky to incriminate himself, not just a little bit, but a lot. I have pure recording gold. This recording is going to probably win an Emmy, it is that good."

"Man, you work fast, that is fantastic," Officer Pierce said and Hubba responded, "Well, there is just one problem, you know how I lead the life of a bachelor, and I don't really clean. There are dishes in the sink from two months ago. You know how I often buy new socks and underwear instead of washing the ones that I have." Officer Pierce responded, "I am sorry, I don't, but I will take your word for it."

Hubba continued, "In order for me to make an anonymous phone call, I have to purchase a burner phone and I have not been that diligent about disposing of the phones when the call is complete. Do you have people that can help me figure out which phone has the recording on it?" Officer Pierce said, "Box em up, send them my way, we will figure out which one is the right one."

"Ummm, there is one more thing," Hubba started, "I may have given Sparky $100,000, my life savings, is there any way that I can get that money back? I had to do that, to get Sparky to talk. You will hear all about it on the phone, once you find it." Unfortunately, because of Federal regulation, this is not something that Officer Pierce could absolutely agree to, but offered to turn a blind eye to Hubba recovering his own money when they arrested Sparky.

Officer Pierce continued, "We don't need you anymore, just do your job as you normally would, try not to draw suspicion, I have a feeling that this will only work if we can surprise Sparky."

The two men made a plan that Hubba would box up the phones with the phony label "Socks and Underwear" and drop them off as a donation for the church. Officer Pierce would stop by the church and pick the phones up there. This transaction would require that Skip, the Pastor of the church, would have to be brought into the plan, even minimally.

Hubba briefed Skip on what was going on giving him just enough information that the church could assist but not enough that Skip would be incriminated by his involvement.

Officer Pierce immediately got in his car and drove to that same church, arriving several hours later where he connected with Pastor Skip, received the box of "socks and underwear."

Returning to Salt Lake City, Officer Pierce began the very time-consuming process of querying each phone to identify the correct recording with his staff of 1 person and his administrative assistant.

They had to find the phone, and assemble the pertinent evidence and plan the arrest.

The FPI, although a federal agency, had not participated in "any" previous raids where arrests were made. There was a fair amount of research that needed to be completed to be successful at the very basic effort of arresting Sparky. It was like bringing the JV middle school football team to the Super Bowl.

The problem for Hubba, Owyhee Kenny, and the whole community of Blackfoot, is that, in this case the JV team was the right team.

The irony of the situation was that Officer Pierce, is a member of both the USDA and the Law Enforcement community. He was feeling very overwhelmed by the plan that he had volunteered for.

Hubba, on the other hand, was feeling better than he had in a long time. It was like the millstone that was around his neck had been removed. He was done with his contribution and now, he had handed everything off to the federal agent.

As free as Hubba felt, there were still some pretty important loops to close.

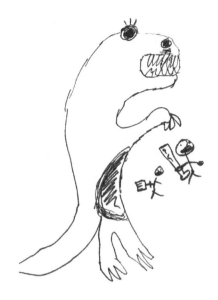

Purple Dinosaur

*The head doesn't come off. The head doesn't
swivel. There's no facial expressions that
can be made. I can only see a certain
amount, because of the peripheral of
Barney's mouth. And when Barney's mouth
is closed, I can't see anything.*
— David Joyner, Actor that played Barney

A bond of trust was formed when he came back
from kidnapping Owyhee Kenny's son Russ. He
stopped by the potato farm on the way home
from work.

Hubba had owned up to his mistakes past
and present. Conversely, Owyhee Kenny knew
that he was also imperfect. He had planned a
tractor accident, allowing it to be pinned on the
very agency that Hubba worked for.

Somehow, in the midst of their filth, these

two men formed a bond of trust. When Owyhee Kenny gave the business card to Hubba and Hubba called the number, the bond was reinforced.

Recognizing that yes, there was still a need to look over his shoulder, Hubba was careful about what he did and where he drove. He didn't take phone calls on unsecured lines. He also knew that he had delivered the most damning piece of evidence about the man and the organization that was causing this level of paranoia. So although careful, Hubba believed that he could travel without suspicion.

The calculus of the situation was this: If things were going to backfire and somehow, through some sort of secret deal with the Devil himself, Sparky was to remain in the community unscathed, then Hubba was a dead man walking. There was no amount of evading interest that would protect him.

His car was his chariot, and Blackfoot, ID felt like his parade grounds. As he drove to Owyhee Kenny's house, he noticed things that he had never seen before. It was like the color had been restored to the buildings and sidewalks. Hubba's spirit for the first time in a long time was free enough to be able to notice it.

He parked in the same tire ruts, now filled with rainwater. He was struck by his own feelings. The last time he was here, he was frighteningly apologetic. Every time before that it was for his job to scare the pants off the entire family.

It was the same tire ruts.

It was the same car.

It was the same physical body.

Something had changed inside of Hubba that made it feel different.

Hubba still had to navigate around the very large metal dinosaur. When he rang the doorbell, he was surprised that Owyhee Kenny was very happy to see him.

Owyhee Kenny had been crying. "Chompers is dead. He was poisoned. Do you know anything about this?"

"No, Nothing. I was working with Officer Kyle Pierce incriminating Sparky."

Then it clicked for both men, Owyhee Kenny said, "It was Sparky, it had to be, that man is a menace, a cancer."

His eyes red and empty of tears, he continued, "Hubba, I am glad to see you," Hubba responded while the two men tried to hug but failed. "Is there someplace a little more private that we can talk?"

Owyhee Kenny said, "We can go down to the pool, it is almost complete. I would like to show it to you anyway. There isn't any water in it, but other than that, it is ready to go. Hold on, let me grab some cups." He didn't grab cups, he grabbed shot glasses and some vodka. Hubba's eyes got big. He didn't want another sip of vodka, ever, but acquiesced because he did not want to risk offending his host and new friend.

The two men leisurely strolled poolside where Owyhee Kenny poured two shots of some cheap vodka. Idaho gets cold in the winter, and both men were wearing large down jackets. It was cold enough that as they talked, their breath escaped syllable by syllable. If it weren't for the vodka, both men would have likely suggested that the conversation continue inside.

Hubba had an idea, "Hold on," he said, and he got up from his pool chair and grabbed an aluminum bat that he had used in his over-forty softball league. Standing on the porch overlooking the pool, he continued "Listen, I feel horrible about this dinosaur, Let's destroy it."

He pulled the bat to his ear, stepped into his stroke and swung the bat into the giant dinosaur. CLANG! The sound of the bat hit the dinosaur, and the force of the swing recoiled and Hubba fell to the ground.

Owyhee Kenny hobbled up the deck and said, "you sure made a loud noise, but left no damage to speak of"

He grabbed the bat, and although he was nursing some broken ribs that were healing, he did his best. The sound was noticeably quieter. He didn't fall and he didn't leave a mark.

"Please give my best to your Crew, Hubba this is a well-constructed Dinosaur." Owyhee Kenny laughed.

This time, Hubba was a man on a mission, he grabbed the bat, and he swung the bat with all of his might, not once, not twice, but as many times as he could muster. It was loud, like the sound that pregnant tuba might make. However, when all was said and done and Hubba drenched with sweat, laying on the deck next to the dinosaur drained entirely of his energy. Almost no physical record on the dinosaur was left.

Laying on the deck, Hubba began to share all that had taken place with Sparky. He told

Owyhee Kenny about the slow-speed chase, the meeting with the FPI. He told him about Sparky, that he gave him some money and the recording. He told him about the SIPC and the Sweet Potato plans. He thanked Owyhee Kenny for his honesty and willingness to forgive after all that had happened to him.

It could have been the vodka, it could have been the total transparency between these two men, but this mention of forgiveness is what prompted Owyhee Kenny, in spite of potentially fraudulent charges, to share.

He was understandably choked up. His voice barely audible, "Hubba, I have something to share with you. Remember that tractor accident that started this whole thing? Well, I set that whole thing up. I removed the governor from the tractor and planned an accident that would just about kill me. I had to. The SIPC was squeezing me so tight that if I hadn't done that, we would have lost our farm. The ironic thing is that it doesn't matter. We are going to lose our farm anyway. The bank is going to foreclose on us."

Hubba was replaying everything that had taken place and his motivation behind his decisions. It had only about thirty seconds of actual time. His brain was a bit foggy from the vodka. It was clear enough to recognize that he had made many life decisions based on some false pretenses. A deep breath, Hubba inhaled precious oxygen into his lungs. This breath signaled he was ready to speak. And then Hubba spoke, "Well.... Crap!"

He stood up, paced around the pool a bit,

and then returned back to the chair. He looked at Owyhee Kenny and said, "I am glad that everything that has taken place has taken place. I don't know if I would have had the courage to undermine Sparky if it hadn't been for the extreme circumstances attached to this situation. Are you going to lose the farm? How bad is it, can we really?"

"I am afraid that a cookie drive and car wash aren't going to help us out, we are pretty deep. We are $100,000 behind on the farm payments. Business hasn't just been bad. It has been anorexic," Owyhee Kenny said.

Hubba immediately blurted out, "$100,000 is the exact amount that I paid Sparky a couple of days ago to get this recording. I would lend that money to you, but it is currently tied up with the SIPC for... I don't know how long, or honestly that I will ever get it back. I mentioned the money to the FPI agent, and he indicated that he would look the other way once the arrest takes place, that is if the arrest took place. Office Pierce still had to find the phone with the incriminating recording on it."

Owyhee Kenny replied "Well ... there it is!" and then the two men laughed it off a bit. The reality is that the money would not have mattered for Owyhee Kenny. For him to get $100,000, it would have only paid for a couple more years, before their farm would be in the exact same place. The suffocating grip of the SIPC had to soften. Something would have to change for Owyhee Kenny to keep his farm. Through Hubba's intervention, something was changing. The very unfortunate outcome for Owyhee Kenny and his family is that any interventions at this point were too late.

Owyhee Kenny thought for a second and finally said, "I have an idea, we may not be able to destroy that dinosaur with a bat, but I do have paint. Let's paint the hell out of that thing."

Two drunk men wandered to the paint shed where they pulled the only paint that was left, blue and red. They poured it into the hopper of the sprayer and began to paint the dinosaur. The men sprayed the metal beast purple. At long last, the vodka had taken its toll and both men laid down and fell asleep for the night, prone on the deck.

 GET TO KNOW IDAHO
The 13-year-old Korean-American girl who sings the song, Baby Shark is from Boise. The song is the 22nd most-popular YouTube video of all time.

The next morning, Dorothea wandered upon two very-hungover men with the hose of a paint-sprayer draped across themselves. She was livid. "You useless blokes have transformed a giant metal dinosaur into Barney." She went on, "Owyhee Kenny, you are lucky that I am committed to the long-term with you because there is a giant purple dinosaur on my porch. I don't usually complain, rubbish piles on top of rubbish and I just adapt, but there is an enormous statue of Barney blocking entry my house." And, Dorothea began to cry.

Hubba, being the perceptive wizard that he was, excused himself and waded through the discomfort on the way to his car.

Hubba waved and drove away fast.

With a crooked smile that won Dorothea's heart, Owyhee Kenny flashed his teeth and said, "Baby, I don't know what happened, we were drinking, and then painting. Barney doesn't matter, you matter, Russ matters! Things may look different, but we are going to get through this."

"What do you mean, look different?" you Dorothea responded, "What are you not telling me?"

Full disclosure

Integrity is telling myself the truth. And
honesty is telling the truth to other people..
— *Spencer Johnson*

Owyhee Kenny sat there, a bit like a deer
trapped in headlights of an oncoming tractor.

He was a storyteller. For him, life was a
story, and he could always reframe something to
the positive. Which he would do even for himself.
He could not control the circumstances, but he
knew that he could control his perspective.

More and more pressure mounted on
Owyhee Kenny to deliver on the success of the
potato farm. He kept reframing the bad news
and kept believing it. The problem was that he
was only sharing the reframed form of the truth
with the people around him.

174

Owyhee Kenny knew that it was time to share, and was now struggling with the guilt of withholding the truth from his wife for as long as he had.

Shaky hands and shaky voice, "Dorothea, things are bad with the potato farm, the SIPC is squeezing us."

Dorothea was innately good at reading people so she knew that things were bad. She also knew that this was not another moment of his schemes. This was his raw vulnerable state.

With eyes of compassion, she tenderly responded, "What do you mean, we are getting squeezed? Isn't this is always what they do? They always apply pressure, we always respond, we are survivors."

Owyhee Kenny answered, "We don't have any fight left. There is no money left. We are leveraged and the only way out is to sell the farm to the SIPC. When they purchased the potato exchange, they got to control the purchase price. Their subsidies have dropped the bottom out of the crop for years. I thought that we could wait it out, in a game of chicken."

Dorothea responded, "So the tractor accident wasn't an accident then. You recklessly put your own life at risk for this."

She had transitioned from the fierce protector and into the betrayed spouse.

Owyhee Kenny responded, "It was not an accident, it was calculated as a way to buy some time. I thought that with a little more time, maybe the SIPC subsidies would dry up, or that we might hit a windfall of cash. I don't know what I thought, in hindsight, it was stupid."

175

"And the bloody pool? Why would you ask for a pool when you knew that we didn't have any money. That was reckless, and stupid" Dorothea responded.

Owyhee Kenny hated to let people down. In this case, there was no other way to reframe it. "I screwed up. I hurt you. I am sorry."

Dorothea has some choices, she loved her husband, and was a fierce protector of this family. This was the greatest mistake that her husband had ever made. He had gone about it alone. If he had shared sooner, she could have at least entered into the problem. In tears, she found her voice, "Is this what you and Hubba were talking about, does he know more about this that your own wife?"

Owyhee Kenny, filled with shame responded, "yes"

Dorothea sat there hurt, sad, angry, befuddled, betrayed, ashamed.

Broken.

She sat in the living room broken. This was yet another consequence of his reckless plan. She was weighing out her next steps. "Should she leave," she kept asking herself. Finally, she was able to muster the words, "I need some time. What else do I need to know?"

Owyhee Kenny also fighting back the tears of shame and guilt shared, "Well, there is one more thing, Hubba was able to get a full recording of Sparky confessing to everything, but.... he lost it. The reality is that even if he could find the recording, it is too late, we cannot whether this storm financially."

"How much time do we have? I mean there

are workers out working on the pool right now applying a vapor-seal liner to your bloody pool.", Dorothea asked.

"A couple of months, maybe and that is if we cut EVERYthing out." Owyhee Kenny responded.

"Bloody Hell!!"

***

Twenty-four hours had passed. Owyhee Kenny knew Dorothea was weighing her future. He could not sleep. He might lose his farm, his wife, his family and his life. He just kept asking himself, "How did I get here?"

 PRO TIP: Crying for long periods of time release oxytocin and endogenous opioids, otherwise known as endorphins.

Finally, Dorothea came back to find her husband, she started, "You hurt me, you were reckless with me and our family. I have spent the last twenty four hours weighing out whether or not I wanted to continue to fight with you and for you. I have decided. I am hurt, but I am in. I want to stay and fight. Circumstances are going to look different, but you are the one that I want to fight with. When I committed to you on our wedding day, I said that I would stand with you for good or for bad, and even though this is bad, you are still the one that I choose."

Owyhee Kenny was paralyzed. He had just

been given the greatest gift, grace.

Grace is an undeserved gift of forgiveness. The greater the pain that you feel for the grievance, the heavier the grace response feels.

"I don't know what to say, I don't deserve your forgiveness, but thank you!" Owyhee Kenny was able to muster.

Dorothea transitioned into the real of what the next couple of months were going to look like. "Well if we are going to move, when do we tell Russ?"

Owyhee Kenny responded, "I think that we have to tell him right away, if we are going to move, we are going to have to pack up our whole life. and that is going to take some time."

Hours passed, and Russ returned home from a sleepover with his friends. The dinosaur was now purple, and his parents were still in the living of their house.

Dorothea started, "Russ we need to talk to you, "We are going to have to move. The potato farm is not making money, and we are in so much debt that we are going to have to move. The SIPC is squeezing tighter than they have ever squeezed before."

She paused to let the bomb that she had just dropped sink in and then continued, "You can't tell anyone. There are a lot of things going on. We have have to protect information, because that protects our family. Over the next couple of months we are going to start packing boxes. I know that you are going to have questions and we will answer anything that we can, but we are asking for your patience and this is going to be the hardest thing that our family has ever faced."

Russ responded, "I knew something was going on, things have been weird, but I am good. I won't tell anyone."

They looked around the house and realized just how much there was to do.

Hash Brown,
RSLH, Esq.

*Someone just asked me why I still needed
cops if the suspect is down and the car is
stopped. I guess cause I have the car keys
and cause he almost killed a dude but I'm
not really sure ?*

— Phoenix Jones
Real-life Super Hero
Seattle, WA, U.S.A.

They devised a plan, they had to get rid of stuff
and pack at the same time. They could not draw
any attention to their efforts. As such, they were
going to use the barn to stage their boxes once
they were packed. This was going to take
months.

The first thing that they wanted to do was
to go through their already stored items and

figure out what they wanted to keep.

Russ brought already packed boxes down from the attic for them to go through to sort and filter.

One box was labelled "Hash Brown, RLSH, Esq."

Neither Dorothea, nor Russ knew was this was. Owyhee Kenny looked up and stated, "There was a time where I may have been masquerading through the streets of Blackfoot as a superhero to keep the streets safe under the pseudonym of Hash Brown"

Dorothea blinked and said, "I'm sorry what? How do I not know about this?"

Owyhee Kenny went on, "I was in high school and there was this thing happening around the country where people would dress up in a superhero costume and keep people safe. So that is what I did in Blackfoot."

Russ, first to respond, blurted out, "Safe from what, rain clouds?"

Owyhee Kenny, both a bit embarrassed by his past and unapologetically stated, "Safe from crime."

Dorothea interjected, "You had a costume?"

Owyhee Kenny responded, "Yes, I had a costume, but there was more. My name was 'Hash Brown, RLSH, Esq.'

 FUN FACT: There are more than a hundred adult real-life superheroes registered on the internet.

As he spoke, he put on the costume, "I was a real-life-superhero" and I was the first of my kind, thus the name. The 'Hash Brown' part was a shout-out to the potato-growing industry. I did have a costume, or at least as way to protect my secret identity."

He put on the gloves, "I wore rubber gloves and sewed together a bunch of burlap potato bags to make a costume."

The gloves fit, the burlap did not. Regardless, he kept squeezing,

"Yes, I had a mask. It covered my hair and my face. It was mostly brown, with some hints of orange, and yellow for effect. The mask was not rigid, it almost looked like a lucha-libre like wrestling mask."

The mask still fit and the burlap was 'mostly' on.

Dorothea added, "Did you have a cape?"

He continued, "A cape, no, I didn't have a cape. He reached into the box and pulled out a manual blender and hung it off of his belt, "I did carry the fiercest looking kitchen tools that I could find."

He pulled out a spatula and hung it on his belt, "you know, it couldn't be a knife. If I carried a knife, that would be considered a deadly weapon. By carrying a spatula, now I was just a citizen walking the mean streets of Blackfoot, keeping things safe."

He added a rolling pin to the holster on his belt, and a flour sieve to a hook.

Russ piled on, "Oh, please tell me that you used these tools in real life and that they did not just hang off your belt."

Owyhee Kenny responded, "Yes, I used the tools while on response."

"Wait, you had a responses?" Russ responded.

"Of course I had responses, I patrolled the streets to keep people safe. There were several incidences. I caught a young thug shoplifting from the Kwik-e-mart. I scared him with the mixer and then used the sieve to detain him until law enforcement could arrive and arrest him."

No one could stop laughing, except Owyhee Kenny. He pulled out the newspaper clipping of the Kwik-e-mart incident Dorothea shared, "I have laughed so hard, that my belly hurts."

Owyhee Kenny concluded by saying, "Please don't tell anyone, the first rule of being a real-life superhero is that you cannot reveal your secret identity, and unfortunately, I did that today. I am sorry for putting you in this place where you have to protect me."

Dorothea looked on, and said, while Russ nodded, your secret will end with me, Hash!"

Spool of Tubing

*Only two things are infinite, the universe
and human stupidity, and I'm not sure about
the former.*

— Albert Einstein

The days went past. Items were being packed;
The process of filtering their lives was long and
emotional.

Russ packed his own things. He continued
to go to school and do his homework. He hung
out with with his friends. No one knew that he
was also concocting a plan to save the family.

On the way home from School, he stopped
by the Potato City Hardware and Screw. He
grabbed two spools of 100 foot vinyl tubing. It
was a large load to carry for a young man, but
certainly not unreasonable.

He got in line to check out. Sparky walked
in. Russ looked away attempting to avoid eye
contact. The cashier in a bit of a Canadian
accent said, "I think that it is terrible what they
are doing to your family"

Sparky interrupted the transaction,

"Excuse me, I understand that I need to sign some invoices."

The cashier responded, "I am with a customer, please feel free to get at the end of the line and I can help people in that order."

Sparky, wouldn't have it, "Look give me the forms and I will just get out of your way, it is pretty simple. You want to help these fine citizens of Blackfoot, just give me my paperwork."

The cashier typed something on his terminal printed out a document and filed it into a pile of docs that Sparky had to sign. He handed Sparky the pile and said, "Sign these."

Sparky signed them all and walked out abruptly.

The cashier laughed. He continued to help Russ, "I will put this on your account."

"Account, I don't have an account," Russ shared.

"You do now, I was mad at Sparky for jumping the line, and for what he has done to your family, so I printed out the paperwork for him to open an account for you. He won't notice, he never looks at anything. It is called pool supplies"

Russ smiled, he didn't like that he was stealing from the SIPC. He felt like the SIPC had been stealing from his family.

The cashier grabbed the first spool of tubing and ran it across the scanner.

"I am guessing that you have some cool science project for this," the cashier said before grabbing the second spooling and scanning that one too.

Russ, not trying to draw attention said, "I do, and am pretty excited about it."

The cashier responded, "That will be $36 on your account today, and anytime you come in go through my register and you can put anything on this account that you want."

 PRO TIP: Generally, three medium russet potatoes or eight to ten small new white potatoes equal one pound.

When he got home, he buried the tubing just under the surface of the ground, deep enough that it would go unnoticed. One end would originate from the basement with the other end stretching as far it could reach. Russ was a smart kid who always trying out new experiments. Russ burying something in the ground was completely normal.

***

Days turned into weeks and for Dorothea and Owyhee Kenny. For both of them it felt really good to be working together toward the same goal. Even though the goal was dismantling the life that they had built together.

In spite of the adversity, they were having a great time together. One day, Owyhee Kenny worked all day in in his Hash Brown mask. Another day, he made a cardboard tombstone for the Idaho Potato that Dorothea had ripped to shreds not so very long ago in the parking lot of the market.

They worked together. They laughed together. It just felt right.

Each day, Russ would stopped at hardware store and bury more tubing.

Taking the Power Back

*Being powerful is like being a lady. If you
have to tell people you are, you aren't.*
— *Margaret Thatcher*

The house was packed with everything non-essential. It was Easter, and the Ibaigurens were expecting a full house of guests. This was the day that Owyhee Kenny was going to share publicly the financial dire that his family was facing. It was Sunday. The farm was about to be foreclosed upon. There were a handful of people and a bank that knew anything. Owyhee Kenny, Dorothea, Russ, Hubba and the First Potato Savings and Loan.

Owyhee Kenny felt responsible for the pile of bills, not because of Sparky and Big Potato, but the mismanagement of what they did have. He could not sell enough potatoes to dig him out of his enormous financial hole. To fill it, you need a shovel, and Owyhee Kenny needed a giant scoop shovel.

The guests had arrived. Owyhee Kenny invited his dear friends. Big Doug, Ms. Yamada, and Hubba were there. Dorothea and Russ were there. Pastor Skip was even there.

Owyhee Kenny decided it was time to share. A portrait of President Washington sat atop the mantle, with what appeared to be an active-listener expression on his face. Ironically enough in all of the packing, a single mobile phone was sitting next to President Washington, which had gone unnoticed in all of the excitement.

Owyhee Kenny wanted to share, and then spend the rest of the day debriefing. Owyhee Kenny stood up and walked to the front of the room and rang a little bell.

As he rang the bell, Dorothea grabbed the phone, and plugged it in to charge.

When you are under pressure, your perception of reality is often incorrect. For Owyhee Kenny, the room felt smaller than it had ever been before. His hands felt larger. He needed to share with these people what was going on, without sharing EVERYTHING. He still could not tell anyone about his responsibility for the tractor accident. The lights began to dim and you could just barely smell the Turkey cooking.

Owyhee Kenny felt like he was standing on the top of the high-ropes challenge course.

189

PRO TIP: On a high-ropes course, always jump for the trapeze, you may miss it, but you won't catch it if you don't jump.

He jumped.

Holding a very large glass of water, he started, "Everyone, I am so glad that you all could make it here today. Easter is a time for us to celebrate being together. Some of you are old friends, some of you are new. All of you are welcome. I have something that I need to share. For many of you, this may not come as a shock. For some, it will be new information. I would like to share and then have a place to talk. I will cut to the chase. We are out of money. I have not been paying the mortgage on the potato farm, mostly because I had to choose between food and mortgage payments, a decision that many other potato farmers before me have had to make. The bank will take possession of the farm, tomorrow. Many of you will immediately turn your anger on the Southeast Idaho Potato Council, and it is probably quite deserved."

Owyhee Kenny took a deep breath and a quick drink of that water to reset. He needed that delay for himself and assumed that everyone listening probably needed a pause as well.

He continued, "I choose to not blame the SIPC; as our situation is a product of industrialization. The small family potato farm cannot compete with the massive scale of industrialized farms. Labor cannot beat

190

machines, ever. Listen, I know that this will impact our Easteer; it will impact what we think about, what we talk about, and plans for the future, it should impact all of those things. Feel free to ask me any questions, and I will do my best to answer them."

The room changed, it went from a close family gathering to a wake after a funeral. People were shocked, they knew that the financial situation was bad, but not "Lose the farm on Monday," bad. Some folks had questions about the newly installed pool and the settlement from the SIPC. These questions Owyhee Kenny handled beautifully. He took ownership, and more importantly, he listened. There were also some very practical questions about where they would live. Owyhee Kenny addressed these as well saying, "The bank knows our situation very well and will let us stay in the house, renting to keep it occupied. We won't be able to farm potatoes here anymore. What does that mean? I will get a job, we will eventually find new housing, life will go on. We will survive because we are together, but frankly, we are starting over."

Young Russ felt helpless. He loved his family and wanted to do something special for them. After his conversation with Ms. Yamada, he had seen the world through a different lens. Despite the rough news that was just delivered by his father, Russ knew it was Easter. Easter meant being together, being thankful and eating. He also knew that he had been planning an Easter gift for the family. Something that he had been working on for some time. Something that now felt very relevant to the situation.

Potatoes can generate power. A fact that Russ had become quite comfortable with since his clock experiment with Ms. Yamada. Russ figured out that he could generate enough power for far more than just a digital clock.

Russ created a network of power producing potatoes, not one, not two, but thousands, each generating a small amount of power, but in a sequence generated enough power to run the entire house: there was a 7 ton HVAC unit, stove, hot water heater, dishwasher. Russ was able to power 30 kWh, enough energy to run all major systems in the house.

 GET TO KNOW IDAHO: The world's first nuclear power plant borders Blackfoot, Idaho. It is also the first power plant to ever have a partial meltdown.

Russ had been collecting potatoes each day for the last three months. When a kid in Blackfoot asks for a potato, you give it to him. When he asks every day, you give him a potato every day. There are never a lot of questions, because well, "Idaho!"

Initial results showed great success and young Russ was reflecting on how everything had turned out magically. He had overridden the standard power inputs to the house without telling anyone. This networked potato grid was his gift to his parents. Easter dinner was going to be delicious and they would never have to pay the power bill again or so he thought. He had made his family cord cutters. Russ was proud!

In Russ's mind, it was unlikely that anyone would wander down the stairs and notice the 5,697 boiled potatoes in the basement. The potatoes were boiled to accelerate the power producing process. The potatoes were beginning to spoil and create a bit of a smell. One rotting potato smells bad, 5,697 rotten potatoes smell like death. Russ, being a smart kid, had thought through the rotten smell and had run 2,486 underground flex tubing vents from the basement. His vents mostly cleared the house of the smell but shared the smell with the rest of the neighborhood for a 3-block radius. The slab had cracks and fissures running through it, so pulling vents was nothing more than pushing some plastic tubing through a hole.

It was game time, all of the planning was done and now it was time to bring the network of potatoes online.

As the potato rot increased rapidly, they stopped producing power, as they could no longer hold the copper and zinc rods that were generating the power. The potatoes were however now producing a highly flammable gas called methane. Because a methane molecule weighs about half as much as that of an oxygen molecule, it was sinking, into the vents and into the neighborhood.

Yes, 911 had been called many times for the smell. No one understood where the smell was coming from. They just knew that the former potato farmland and neighboring houses smelled a bit like the Cambodian killing fields. Emergency services were sent out, police, fire, ambulance. To be clear, methane by itself does not create a smell, it was the rot of the potatoes that was funneling through the vents.

And then it happened, a spark hit the methane gas and immediately caught fire. It was one of the Ibaiguren's neighbors, which ironically there were not many. The neighbor in question was named Craig. A classic Good ol'boy with small-town charm. He was deep-frying his turkey in peanut oil.

For all intents and purposes of this story, Craig was invented for a single purpose, which will become evidently clear in the next two paragraphs.

 PRO TIP: One-dimensional characters have a single purpose. Real people never have a single purpose.

Craig had finished a six-pack of beer and was on to his second open six-pack of beer. While holding this beverage, Craig was wearing a hat that read, "Wild Stallions" and a sweatshirt that read, "Stay classy Easter." Craig did not care what people thought of his shirt or hat. He didn't care what people thought of him. Craig cared about one thing, deep-frying his turkey.

Coupled with the beer, Craig had gotten a bit existential. Somehow he needs to release the spirit of the turkey while boiling its carcass in oil.

To ensure that the turkey would get fully fried, Craig added extra oil and set the heat source to "High" I believe Craig's "Two six-packs in" inebriated words were "we're gonna set this bird free, FREE, FREEBIRD!" Which then prompted Craig to sing loudly. There he was, in his backyard, drunk as a skunk, singing "Free as a bird," dancing, while circling, paying homage to the bird he was about to fry.

And then, after sufficiently appeasing the Gods of Easter turkeys, Craig lowered his lifeless bird carcass into the vat of boiling peanut oil. The bird was set free, and not a little bit either. As you can imagine, when Peanut oil boils over and hits the flame of the propane burner, a chemical reaction is created and you have made fire. Yes, there was fire and a lot of it. The rapid boil created a bit of an explosion, shooting hot, fiery oil in every direction. And yes, the fiery oil splashed onto one of the methane vents translating Craig's now prophetic phrase into what can only be described as Dresden firebombing on this unsuspecting neighborhood. That bird was free!

He paused, staring at the giant fire, and a single tear formed in his right eye and he whispered, "I did it, Tom Turkey is free."

If it had been nighttime, then the light from each individual vent would have produced enough light to make it shine like the day. Enough light to illuminate a three-block radius.

Confusion in the area was running rampant. No one knew what was going on. Craig stood there looking at the fryer, and the fire. Ironically his turkey had been cooked in record time but he was too melancholy to eat it. His universe stopped and the earth opened to celebrate his victory. In retrospect, this was not the view held by everyone that day.

In fact, Russ and his family were completely unaware that any of it was going on. They only knew that the stove was no longer working, the HVAC had slowed, and the lights were flickering.

After re-hearing the news from his father about their dire financial situation, Russ was depressed. He went to his room to get his thoughts in order. He laid down on his bed for a second to recount what he had just heard. Sure enough, he fell asleep in his room recounting the details. He hadn't planned on a nap, but sometimes the body needs what the body needs. After Russ was asleep, he had no idea about anything that was going on in the neighborhood.

Law enforcement started to evaluate the situation and arrived at a theory. The flames that were shooting 8 feet in the air in a perfectly concentric circle. It seemed that each flame was pointing at the middle. The center of the circle was the potato farm of Owyhee Kenny. This was either a clear sign of an alien attack, or there was something inside the circle that needed to be investigated. The Police would either arrive at the source of the blaze OR be the first to make alien contact. Initially, there was just a single police car that had responded, shortly after more arrived on the scene together with a slew of fire trucks.

You could hear from the first responder still screaming, "Sweet Potato!"

When the fire department arrived, they made quick work of handling the fire. They pulled the hoses out of the fire trucks. It was like a giant ant colony, each doing their own thing, not talking to each other, just working. Hoses were pulled out, Trucks were positioned just so, and then the water started to spray.

There was enough water to reduce the flames enough for a person to get through. One of the policemen jumped through the opening in the wall of fire. Then the water stopped, while intelligence was gathered. The policeman started to walk. He didn't know where he was going, but he knew that he only had three blocks that he could walk in and there was plenty of light to guide his way.

As he walked, he eventually stumbled upon a house in the dead center, where the lights were flickering. People were in the living room, completely unaware that anything was going on around them.

Ironically someone had cued up "Ring of Fire" by Johnny Cash on the stereo. As the officer walked up to the house he heard the lyrics "And it burns burns burns, the ring of fire, the ring of fire." The officer knocked loudly on the door.

"Howdy Neighbor, Happy Easter!" said a voice as the door opened, the officer parroted back "Happy Easter." After a prolonged, uncomfortable delay, the officer asked, "What is going on here?"

"Well we are not quite sure, the oven stopped working, the lights started to flicker and the house is cold. It is, however, Easter." At that moment Dorothea came looking for Russ, "Hey where is Russ?" She said,

Owyhee Kenny responded back, "What? check his room, maybe he is taking a nap, Go get him, he needs to be a part of this" Dorothea went upstairs to wake the young man and bring him downstairs.

Owyhee Kenny looked back at the officer standing on his porch and blinked a few times trying to remember the conversation that they were having. He finally said, "How can I help you tonight officer?"

At this moment, Russ wandered downstairs and onto the deck where he quickly sized up the situation and realized the lights were flickering because of the potatoes in the basement. This is when Russ addressed the family.

"Hey everyone, I have an announcement. As many of you know, I have been really into science and potatoes lately. I also have been trying to figure out how to reduce our dependence on fossil fuels and I think that I have it figured it out.

Potatoes.

Potatoes are the key to breaking the stronghold cartel of foreign oil and that is why I have created a grid of networked potatoes in our basement, each in sequence creating enough electricity to power our home. Clearly, something has gone wrong in my plan. This should be an easy fix. I will go down to the basement, fix the potato that is misbehaving and we are still going to have a Happy Easter."

The officer was dumbfounded; Jaw

dropped to the floor and he was looking on in amazement about what he had just heard. The entire house was fueled by potatoes. He had not drawn the connection that the fire pandemonium in the streets had been caused by a science project gone awry. That is until Russ opened the door to the basement, and the smell of warm potato decay climbed into Russ's nostrils. This moment is the moment in Russ's life when he knew that there was a problem and it was big. He immediately shut the door and went back out to the deck for his next announcement.

"I have made a huge miscalculation; I was not generating enough power with standard potatoes so I boiled 5,697 potatoes before creating the NPG (Networked Potato Grid). A boiled potato can create 5 times the power of a non-boiled potato, so in order for me to generate enough from the NPG, I had to boil them. What I hadn't thought through was that a boiled potato will spoil much more quickly than a non-boiled potato. One spoiled potato is not a big deal, 5,697 creates a lot of heat creating a logarithmic warming trend. The warmer that it got in that basement the faster that the potatoes spoiled. I have thought through the smell, which is why I laid 2,486 vents from the basement, each exactly 3/10 of a mile long, creating a circle around our house.

The idea was that three blocks would be enough distance from the house that the smell would not be all concentrated in a single spot, so no one has to smell the power of chemistry.

This is the point in time where the officer

made the connection. 3/10 of a mile in a circle. "Excuse me, Russ, what in your chemistry might cause flames coming out of that circle and burn continuously?"

Russ thought about it. "Methane. Why?"

"Well because the neighborhood is on fire," the officer responded.

A deep flood of awareness overcame young Russ. Everyone makes mistakes but not everyone's mistakes light an entire neighborhood on fire. Awareness quickly transitioned into panic, and from panic into distress.

Immediately the power grid was disabled and then Owyhee Kenny leaped up and ran through the house to the spigot where the water supply is kept; he went and turned his water supply on. He dragged a hose to the basement. Then he dragged another hose, and another and another until every hose on the potato farm was pointed down the stairs into the basement of the Ibaiguren Family Potato Farm.

It was fitting that the water, the clean water, the water that Dorothea's father had purified when he had installed the filtration system at their potato farm was pouring down the stairs. It was 99.9999% pure and flowing down the stairs into the basement suffocating the methane gas in an attempt to control the burn. Once the potatoes were covered in water, the gas was not being released into the air, and the fire would no longer have fuel.

Now the basement was flooded with water, each of the flaming geysers was extinguished one at a time. Each vent was removed and the immediate danger was handled. Although the fire was out, and the situation was under control, there was still a very real issue of a basement full of rotten potatoes, water, and whatever else was down there.

And then, after what can only be described as the most exciting night that Blackfoot had ever seen, people went to bed and opted to clean the whole thing up in the morning.

The Takedown

*So many battles waged over the years, and
yet none of them like this, are we destined to
destroy each other, or can we change who
we are, and unite, is the future truly set?*
   - Professor Xavier, X-men,
          Days of Future Past

Nothing had changed for Owyhee Kenny and his
family. They were still out of money. They were
still going to have to give the potato farm back to
the bank. The Southeast Idaho Potato Council
had won. This is probably why Owyhee Kenny
wasn't angry with Russ. The Easter guests had
stayed the night and helped put out the fires.
They cleaned the house enough to be inhabited.

Power was restored to the electrical panel and work began.

They all awoke around sunrise and they knew that they had a lot of work ahead of them. Quiet murmurs echoed through the farm. No one wanted to clean it up, but it was the right thing to do.

It was the day after Easter.

News travels fast in a small town. Anyone who hadn't heard about the commotion the night before certainly had heard about it by now. Instead of going to the stores to buy new scented candles and large screen televisions, they had instead found their way to a potato farm that the night before had been ablaze and visible from outer space.

The Southeast Idaho Potato Council was under federal investigation by the United States Department of Agriculture. The agent, Kyle Pierce had been riddled with more than one hundred phones and was attempting to find incriminating evidence on the head of the Potato Mafia, a.k.a. Big Potato, a.k.a. the Southeast Idaho Potato Council. There were only three men who knew about this person and his unknown department shared between the USDA and Law Enforcement. Generally, no one doubted that Kyle Pierce was in fact who he said that he was, but there were some questions as to whether or not he was over his head and would be able to take down the SIPC. Even if the incriminating audio recording was to be found.

Hubba had "invested" $100,000 in the SIPC and the plans to shut down all potato industry in the area. Hubba, Sparky, and

Owyhee Kenny were the only people in the world that knew about this. Hubba had clearly picked his allegiance and it was only a matter of time before Sparky found out.

Hubba would pay dearly for his sins. If the FPI couldn't pull through, Hubba, for good reasons believed that he would not only lose the money that he had invested, but that he would minimally be banished from town, but more likely, his life was at risk.

Only the people who were in the room before the Easter dinner and the bank knew the absolute dire financial state of the Ibaiguren Potato farm.

As the sun rose higher in the sky, the crowd outside the potato farm grew larger and larger. There were neighbors who wanted to know more, there were well-wishers who knew the family and wanted to be supportive, and there were many lookie-loos rubberneckers who just wanted to get a glimpse at this very historic moment in their town's history.

Right around 10:30 a.m., a car pulled up to the farm. It took some time to find a spot because there were already cars parked everywhere. Inside the car was a very giddy Sparky. He did not know any of the back-story at this point. He only knew that the only farm that was standing in the way between him and his dream of replacing all potato farms with sweet potato farms had just almost lit the entire town on fire the night before.

When Hubba saw Sparky's car park, he looked for cover. He felt like he had to hide, he disappeared into the crowd of people that were there to observe this very large local event.

Sparky walked his way to the front of the crowd, and straight up to Owyhee Kenny who was still wearing a bit of a back brace.

Sparky asked Owyhee Kenny, "What happened here, it looks like there was a fire, is everyone okay? Is the farm okay, will you still be able to grow potatoes? What is going on?" Sparky appeared concerned but it was clear that his emotion was completely self-serving. At this point, Owyhee Kenny literally had nothing left. He couldn't think fast enough to counter Sparky's maneuverings. He was out of gas emotionally. His family farm, the homestead, had just about burned to the ground. The bank was about to repossess it and he was exhausted.

Without much pomp or circumstance, Owyhee Kenny started to speak. The second that he opened his mouth, the standing room only festival-like crowd went silent so that they could hear what was being said. While Owyhee Kenny spoke, you could hear the occasional whisper as information was being passed back through the crowd.

Owyhee Kenny said, "You win, the SIPC wins. We are out of money, not a little bit out of money, we are entirely out of money. You and the SIPC have squeezed all the juice out of the lemon. We are going to have to give our farm back to the bank. We, like so many farmers before us, were squeezed, coerced, and threatened out of an honest and fair wage for honest and fair work. Your organization has slowly by slowly taken over every aspect of this community. We see the local price of potatoes dropping. We know that the SIPC is setting that price. We, the potato farmers can't afford to buy shoes for our kids. Meanwhile, the potato exchange is lining its pockets with potato-blood money. I am done. I quit. I cannot fight you any longer. I cannot fight the SIPC any longer. On Monday, I am going to the bank and I will sign over the deed to the farm. You win. I lose, but more importantly, the whole community loses.

Skip, the pastor from the church, and a Easter guest was a skilled orator and gifted at spontaneous diatribes. He came forward and addressed the crowd. Many of the people in the crowd were people from his church. Skip projected his voice, "People of Blackfoot, thank you for coming today. Many of you came to support Owyhee Kenny and his family, others of you came because you heard that there was a fire and you wanted to see the carnage. I don't care why you came. The important thing is that you came. I believe that we as a community can come alongside this family, which has been a cornerstone of this community and share some of the thankfulness that we have for them. They haven't had to hang on to their farm for as long as they have, it has been a choice. They have held onto the dream that so many of us held but gave up on when we were faced with the decision to fight the SIPC or quit and move on. Listen, I am going to put together a signup form. Owyhee Kenny and his family need $100,000 to be able to get out from under this burden from the bank. I am going to start a fund right now. I am going to put $5,000 into this fund, and I am going to encourage each of you to figure out how much you can put in as well. Maybe you can only give $50 this year, but that is $50 that will help keep this way of life, the way of the small family farm, still running. Come over and see me and let me know what you can do."

As you can imagine, after Owyhee Kenny's and Skip's speeches, Sparky was absolutely ecstatic and then worried. Success was so close that he could taste it. As the words were coming out of Owyhee Kenny's mouth, all Sparky could hear was: "You win, you win, you win, you win, you win." Not a single other word landed. He was enjoying his state of euphoria until he heard $5,000 fund and "give money." Suddenly Sparky was very aware of what was going on.

As Skip was working the crowd, a black F-150 Pickup Truck pulled up and parked. Two of the truck's side windows had a handwritten sign that said "FPI." The sign was clearly affixed and in plain sight per federal codes on vehicles that make arrests. No one noticed the truck's arrival, but even if someone had noticed the truck, it would not have been completely unheard of for a federal response from the United States Department of Agriculture to respond to the events that had taken place on this property the night before. Kyle Pierce was present to tell Hubba that he could not find the recordings on any of the phones that were shared with him. This felt like the kind of thing one would do in person. Officer Pierce had prepped to make an arrest today, but without the recording, his trip was just an inspection.

This situation became especially tricky for Hubba, as he was now an investor in the Sweet

Potato excitement and the only thing that cleared him of liability was the recording on that phone. Hubba had cooperated with the FPI, and the only thing that would send Sparky to jail was on that phone and without it, Hubba was in great danger.

Office Pierce knew this. This connection was the exact reason that he drove to the family potato farm. He wanted to share what had taken place in person. Kyle Pierce and a woman is dressed in blue stepped out of the truck, walked across the street, and assimilated into the crowd. There was a lot of energy there. Folks were still concerned about what had taken place the night before. They were concerned for the family and they were frustrated with the SIPC.

Skip was working the crowd, writing things downs, clarifying. People were making phone calls and were giving as much as they could give. He walked right past Officer Pierce without recognizing him. In total, it took Skip about fifteen minutes to record everyone's commitments. He addressed the crowd one more time. He said, "Friends, look I know that times are hard, and many of you have already committed to as much as you can, but we have $42,000 committed, and we need $100,000 to be able to help this family keep their potato farm. There may be other folks in the community that can help, but look, we are near the end." At this moment, Skip got a bit of a sparkle in his eye. He looked right at Sparky and said, "Maybe the Southeast Idaho Potato Council could help this family. Would the SIPC be willing to match the commitments made so that this family could keep their potato farm? It is good for the community. That would leave just $8000 to raise."

At that moment, Sparky, without hesitation, responded, "In a word, no. We are not going to help this family. When this farm goes back to the bank, the SIPC will purchase the farm from the bank for pennies on the dollar. We will then own all potato farms in all of Southeast Idaho. I have worked all of my adult life for this to happen and I want this farm, I need this farm." At this point in his diatribe, Sparky had not yet incriminated himself.

 PRO TIP: Do not ever reveal your evil plans publicly. Many evil villains have come before you and done just that, but they always get caught.

Taken aback, Skip looked Sparky squarely in the eye and said, "We are going to raise this money, you are going down. Sweet dreams, Sweet Potato!"

It was at this moment that Dorothea grabbed the now charged cell phone which had exactly one voice recording on it. Hoping with fierceness of a mother protecting her family she interrupted the hullabaloo by playing the recording on the outside speakers. It was the recorded conversation between Hubba and Sparky.

Officer Pierce shouted, "Sparky, you are under arrest!"

His ears had perked up as he was listening to Sparky incriminate himself over the loud-speaker. He thought this is probably the best time to arrest this man. He had been listening to the entire diatribe, and Sparky had just incriminated himself.

Officer Pierce had been studying guidelines for making arrests as a federal agency. So he knew what to do. After his exclamation, everyone was looking at him. He and his partner waded through the crowd to the front where Skip, Sparky, and Owyhee Kenny were standing. He brushed against Hubba, hiding in the crowd, and didn't notice. Hubba took the opportunity to follow Officer Pierce to the front. Adrenaline was rushing through both men's bodies. Hubba was about to out himself as the traitor and Officer Pierce had never made an arrest before. This was a nervous euphoria.

When he finally reached the front, he held out his freshly minted badge created for just such an arrest. Instead of a shield, it was a potato, baked with a scroll across it that read, "FPI." Above the potato, it read, "Federal Potato Investigators," and below the potato, it read "A Division of the United States Department of Agriculture."

He said "Sparky, my name is Kyle Pierce. I am a Federal Agent with the Federal Potato Investigators, a department of the United State Department of Agriculture, and you are under arrest for the following." Yes, he had a list. He had transcribed his list onto a notecard.

PRO TIP: As a federal agent, memorize the list of infractions. When you are reading from a notecard, you lose credibility.

"Extortion, intimidation, price gouging, kidnapping, coercion, corruption, Insurance Fraud and the kicker under Federal Market Order 945 section 'E', Subsection '2,' Paragraph 'i' and 'ii', it states, *'Export: Except potatoes of a size not smaller than 1/2 inches in diameter may be shipped if the potatoes grade not less than U.S. No. 2; and (ii) Prepeeling: Except potatoes of a size not smaller than 1 1/2 inches in diameter may be shipped if the potatoes grade not less than Idaho Utility or Oregon Utility grade.'*

And your unpeeled potatoes are consistently falling short of the 1 ½ inch diameter."

"Boom, we got you!"

Sparky was dumbfounded and said, "You have got to be kidding me. I have never heard of the Federal Potato Investigators. There is no way that that badge is real. This has to be pretend land." Officer Pierce replied while continuing to show his badge, "No this is real, and to be honest, we don't make a lot of arrests in the FPI." Sparky looked at his officer who was on the payroll and saw that he was just finishing up a phone call. The officer glanced back at Sparky and said, "Everything checks out, he is legit, you are being arrested by the FPI today, it is a division of the USDA."

Hubba and Sparky's eyes met. Sparky had

some confusion as to why Hubba was now present. The thought of betrayal had just entered his mind, and as the seconds ticked by, the reality of the betrayal became more and more obvious, and then Hubba confirmed it. "Sparky, I have known you since we were little kids. You helped save my mother of her terminal illness, but ever since that day, you have lorded that over me. You have wreaked havoc on this town, on these people, on me. You have asked me to do things that I can't undo. I have broken local, state, and federal laws for you, all because I felt like I had to. When I met Kyle Pierce, the FPI agent, I knew that there was an out, so yeah, I talked to him, and told him everything. The FPI knows everything and you are going away for a very long time."

At this point, Sparky knew that he was done for, so he attempted to run, but in a twist of irony reserved for literature, Sparky ran smack dab into an enormous metal painted-purple barney. He hit the metal statue so hard that he fell to the ground and was knocked unconscious. Ironically, his collision dented the giant metal beast, something Hubba and Owyhee Kenny were unable to do.

When he awoke, Sparky was getting handcuffed. Hands shaking, Officer Pierce flipped to his second note card and started to read "You have the right to remain silent, anything that you say can and will be used against you in the court of law." Officer Pierce continued, but Sparky couldn't hear anything, no one could, there was a sense of disbelief about what had just taken place.

Sparky was then escorted to the F-150 where he would be transported to detainment facility in Salt Lake City, Utah. There were only two seats in the cab of the truck and there were now three people traveling so Sparky would ride in the tailgate.

When Sparky walked past Hubba, he verbalized, "I should have let your mother die."

Sparky was loaded into the tailgate of the truck, still handcuffed. Officer Pierce and his partner got into the cab of the truck and drove away.

There was a sense of heaviness that had just been lifted off the community. An over-lordish grip had been removed and a collective sigh of relief could be breathed. The only problem was that with Sparky gone, the SIPC still owned everything in town and this family was still going to lose the farm.

Owyhee Kenny spoke up, "Well that is not something that I expected to see in my lifetime. We as a community are going to heal. Everything is going to be different, but we get to choose what that "difference" is. The SIPC still controls everything. There will just be new people in control. We have a lot of work to do to figure out exactly what is going to happen next. I know for a fact that the 'next' thing for me is to clean up this mess. Anyone willing to stay and help clean up would be greatly appreciated."

Neighbors, friends, and family all stayed around to help. People started to move debris and fire-singed materials. The house was being aired out. People went to get their wet-dry vacs and their dehumidifiers. A lot had taken place, but in the true spirit of small-town America, everyone pitched in and started working.

The Myopic Rise and Fall of the Southeast Idaho Potato Council

2 Sam. 23:13-17
David had a craving and said, "Oh that someone would give me water to drink from the well of Bethlehem which is by the gate!" So the three mighty men broke through the camp of the Philistines, and drew water from the well of Bethlehem which was by the gate, and took it and brought it to David. Nevertheless, he would not drink it, but poured it out to the Lord; and he said, "Be it far from me, O Lord, that I should do this. Shall I drink the blood of the men who went in jeopardy of their lives?" Therefore he would not drink it. These things the three mighty men did.
- New International Version

It was the water. It was always about the water. The water filtration system that Dorothea's father had given the newlyweds when they were first married is what caused Owyhee Kenny's potatoes to win first prize each year at the Bingham County Fair. The water that stabilized the great Easter potato power incident. And it is the water that saved the family potato farm.

How did it save the family potato farm?

Well, when life gives you lemons, you make lemonade. When life gives you a basement full of potato mash that is mixed with the purest water in Idaho and yeast, well then you have vodka or you have the beginning of vodka. You have what is called a mash.

Alcohol is produced when yeast feasts on the sugars in the mash. Cane sugar produces rum, Agave produces tequila and potato sugars, produce vodka. As soon as the yeast that Dorothea stored in the basement was mixed with the potatoes and water, alcohol was being produced and at an incredible volume.

When everyone started, they needed to do something about the basement. The community showed up to work. Pastor Skip, members of the church, even Mr. Potato Head himself, Hubba, showed up to help clean up the mess. They needed a plan because although many hands make light work, many hands that don't have a plan, just create a lot of confusion.

The solution to the basement full of some toxic liquid was to fill that new swimming pool. The pool was empty, or mostly empty. Because they were draining a highly volatile liquid, they wanted to reduce any chance of a chemical reaction. They used gravity to drain the basement of the water and dump the water in the basement into the pool. Pumps were used to empty the pool completely and suction kept pulling water out until it was empty. The emptying of the pool process took a while..

Once the pool was empty and cleaned, the water in the basement was emptied into the pool. Hoses were run from the basement and directly to the pool. Once the hoses were in place, the liquid was allowed to drain.

 GET TO KNOW IDAHO: In Rigby, Pilo Farnsworth invented the television. He was inspired plowing a potato field, the parallel rows triggering his notion of television scan lines.

Now keep in mind that this was no small pool. It was very large, purchased and paid for by Big Potato. As the water of the basement was being emptied into the pool, Pastor Skip arrived. He was a caring man and was always willing to help. He knew that there was a large clean up taking place. Pastor Skip walked up to the house. Promptly turned around, walked back to his car.

There was a lot of energy, people buzzing about, so no one noticed today's arrival of Pastor Skip and his subsequent departure. There was a job board hung up outside the house, and when new people got there, they checked the job board. When people left, there was no checking out. You just moved on. Regardless, people were constantly coming and going all day long.

Immediately Skip walked back to the house carrying a cup with "Snagglepuss" on it. He lowered his mug into the pool water and pulled out a cup of liquid. Skip pressed the cup to his lips and murmured something like "There it is, come to daddy."

Skip was in a bit of a daze for about 30 seconds until he awoke from his trance and finally realized what had just happened. He inquired, "Owyhee Kenny, why is your pool full of the best vodka mash that I have ever tasted."

For a moment, Owyhee Kenny stood there stunned. He then went immediately pale. Owyhee Kenny was no longer with us. He had transcended to the spirit world where he was calculating how his pool ended up full of vodka.

There was a lot of activity around the pool at that moment. Skip went on to share his discovery with folks milling about, and even Hubba, who was helping with cleanup tasted the vodka. And there was a moment for each one of them as they realized exactly what had happened.

Now it is interesting that it was the Pastor that was able to sniff the vodka out of the swimming pool, but there was no judgment toward him then, and there is no judgment at present. There is respect for Pastors that smell out a good vodka. In the Bible, Jesus had turned water into the best wine for a party, so, Salut!

After a couple of minutes, Owyhee Kenny started to come down out of his trance, but not too quickly.

The realities of the situation started to add up. A bottle of vodka that could be sold for

$100/bottle and the pool was 40 feet long by 20 feet wide with an average depth of 7.5 Ft, which after applying some quick math into the situation, It means...

Length x Width x Average Depth x 7.5
= Total gallons

There were 42,000 gallons of vodka and there were five bottles of vodka in a gallon, at the sale price of $100 per bottle. This is a reasonable price for a high-end bottle of vodka, meant that there was $21,000,000 dollars worth of vodka sitting in that... there... swimming pool.

Additionally, there was a warehouse full of clean bottles that were donated to the church sitting in a warehouse to help cover the family's medical bills.

Skip, without missing a beat, immediately walked out to his car, went straight to the moving truck rental place and rented a truck, which he could take to the warehouse that was housing all of the donated bottles. Skip drove to the warehouse where he loaded the truck in just under 30 minutes.

He drove the truck slowly, carefully over to the Ibaiguren's house. By the time Skip arrived at the house, news had spread to everyone that there was a lot of vodka in the pool. Skip backed the moving truck up to the pool. He got out of the truck, opened the sliding back door and said, "Everyone, we have bottles! After the accident, at church, we started a bottle drive to help support the needs of this family. Little did we know that the bottles would fill this need."

To which Owyhee Kenny responded, "You have bottles, for alcohol? How many?"

"A whole warehouse full," Skip playfully replied.

Owyhee Kenny slowly mouthed, while adding a dramatic pause for effect, "a whole warehouse full... FULL, really?" The mash would need to be distilled to become real vodka, but the reality was just starting to set in.

Make no mistake, this moment was without question a moment set apart from all other moments. It was a wrinkle in the cosmos, the stars and moon had come into alignment. This was not random, and it was not by chance. It was no cosmic coincidence or happenstance. There was an injustice, and to restore balance, the universe groaned and required it. Regardless of your faith background, it was clear this pool of vodka happened for a reason. And that reason was to restore a family and a community back to prominence. The yin always needs a yang.

And then, Skip grabbed the first empty bottle and grabbed one of the empty hoses, created suction and filled the bottle with vodka. He put the cap on the bottle, looked up from his creation, and said, "These bottles will not fill themselves, we have a lot of work to do, and the Good Lord in Heaven knows that I am NOT going to fill these bottles by myself." And everyone jumped in, grabbed a bottle and started to fill.

One by one, the bottles were filled with vodka mash and put back into the truck. The truck would return to the warehouse and a new truck would show up. It was an around the clock operation. Folks would show up. Folks would leave. Trucks would show up. Trucks would leave.

In total, the operation to fill the bottles took the better part of four days. When the last bottle was filled, a gasp of exhaustion fell on the crowd. Owyhee Kenny, Dorothea, Russ, Skip, Ms. Yamada, Hubba had all been working bottling non-stop, taking only short breaks to sleep.

There were Cairns in every direction for as far as the eye could see. There was a community recovering from the myopic rise and fall of the Southeast Idaho Potato Council. The swimming pool was empty again and there was a large purple metal T-Rex on the front porch and numerous other remnants of the SIPC scattered across the farm.

And then, Pastor Skip humbly grabbed two bottles of vodka mash. He was exhausted from the emotional ride since Easter. He had one bottle in his left hand, and one in his right hand. He took the bottle in his left hand, cleared his throat, and said, "This bottle- is a bottle of remembrance. We will remember this day as the day that the God of the Universe rescued this family, their farm, and this community. From the Bible, in Second Samuel, there was a point where King David was holed up in a cave by his enemy, and he sent his men, at great risk, to get water from the far gate. His men braved death to get the water and then returned it to the cave where David was." At this point, Skip took the cap off the bottle and began to pour it out. He then continued, "David offered this water up, the water his men risked their lives to collect, as a sacrifice, a liquid offering. Today, this vodka is a liquid offering. It is for us. It is for God, it is for everyone who sacrificed for this community."

Skip then took the cap off the second bottle and said, "This bottle is for us to drink. Let us celebrate this moment." And he passed the bottle.

They celebrated.

About This Book

and us

This story started in the oral tradition of storytelling. Each night before bed, and on the way to school. Stories are shared. The story of Russ is one of those stories. It all started with rewiring the house with potatoes and grew from there into the story that is here today. There are the voices of all five of our children echoing in the words written here. Each sharing what they had to offer. Thank you for reading and entering into the storytelling of our family.

My daughter Raffaella drew all of the chapter headings, and her imagination and creativity inspired me.

My eldest son Eli, was my best editor. He would call me out on things that just weren't believable. He would give me the hard truth that no one else could. You know, "This part really, really sucks!"

My son Eben listened to me carry-on about plot points.

My daughter Betti and my son Noah, both just got caught up in the excitement of the story.

And then, there is my bride, Jessica who puts up with story after story, idea after idea and loves me because of it.

I should mention there are names of people that we know in this book. It is neither a coincidence nor an allegation. All characters are composite personalities and are a byproduct of family stories and bits and pieces of folklore and legend.

Our family lives on Signal Mountain in Tennessee, where we, with the help of some brilliant people, started a technology company called AudiencePoint. Prior to moving to Tennessee four years ago, we lived in Port Townsend, Washington, a place that will always live in our hearts as home.

Our connection to Idaho? My wife Jessica grew up in Boise (boy-see), a place that we love and visit as often as we can.

The following is a picture of our family, including a random bird photo-bombing, drawn by Betti Shriner, while Age 6.

Made in the USA
Monee, IL
11 December 2019